Joseph Wallace

Sketch of the Life and Public Services of Edward D. Baker

United States Senator From Oregon

Joseph Wallace

Sketch of the Life and Public Services of Edward D. Baker
United States Senator From Oregon

ISBN/EAN: 9783337010409

Printed in Europe, USA, Canada, Australia, Japan

Cover: Foto ©Raphael Reischuk / pixelio.de

More available books at **www.hansebooks.com**

SKETCH

LIFE AND PUBLIC SERVICES

OF

EDWARD D. BAKER,

UNITED STATES SENATOR FROM OREGON,

AND FORMERLY REPRESENTATIVE IN CONGRESS FROM ILLINOIS,
WHO DIED IN BATTLE NEAR LEESBURG, VA.,
OCTOBER 21, A. D. 1861.

———

——— " Who trod the ways of glory,
And sounded all the depths and shoals of fame."
SHAKESPEARE.

———

By JOS. WALLACE.

———

.

SPRINGFIELD, ILL.:
——
1870.

JOURNAL COMPANY,
PRINTERS AND BINDERS,
SPRINGFIELD, ILL.

PREFACE.

From time immemorial, it has been a custom with the noble fraternity of authors, whenever they offered a new book to the reading public, to preface it with such remarks, explanatory and apologetic, as might be deemed best to secure the favorable attention of that public. 'In accordance with this time-honored usage, the writer of the present sketch, before introducing his hero directly to the reader, begs leave to offer a word of explanation.

The principal portion of the following memoir, with others of eminent Illinoisans, was prepared, by the writer, about the close of our late civil war, with the view to a joint publication; but that idea having been temporarily abandoned, he now offers this little work to the public in a separate form.

A number of fugitive notices and obituaries of Colonel Baker appeared in the newspapers of the country, at the time of his death, and, soon thereafter, a well written biographical article from the ready pen of Mr. John Hay, (present secretary of American Legation at the Court of Madrid,) which was printed in Harper's Magazine for December, 1861. Other brief sketches, more or less accurate, are also to be found in the late Encyclopedias, and among the various historical records of the Rebellion. Nothing, however, in the shape of an extended narrative, has hitherto been published of one, whom, in life, the nation willingly honored. To supply, in some measure, what, in this respect, seems to be a public want, is the object of the present volume—a work which, while making no pretensions to the character of a full and elaborate biography, is, nevertheless, the most complete of any previously produced of its gifted and lamented subject. The writer has aimed to write not as a partisan, but to portray the MAN just as he was; letting him speak for himself upon the great questions dividing public sentiment in his day.

The eulogies of Hon. O. H. Browning, of Illinois; of the late Hon. James A. McDougall, of California, and of Hon. Schuyler Colfax, of Indiana, delivered in the Congress of the United States, on the occasion of the formal announcement of Senator Baker's demise, are, in themselves, fine oratorical productions, and constitute a valuable portion of this book. They are inserted in the form of an appendix at the close of the sketch.

The photographer of the likeness of Colonel Baker, which precedes the title page, is Mr. Isaac H. Voorhis, of Springfield, Ill.—the picture being copied from an elegant steel portrait in the hands of Dr. William Jayne, of this city.

With these introductory remarks, and without undertaking to apologize for its many imperfections and deficiences, the writer submits his work, with whatever of merit it does possess, to the candor of those who may choose to read it.

SPRINGFIELD, February 1st, 1870.

ERRATA.

On page 14, 6th line of the last paragraph, for *Broad Axe River*, read *Bad Axe River*.

Page 51, next to last line of the first paragraph, for *gray bald*, read *good gray*.

Page 56, 4th line of the last paragraph, for *leader*, read *leaders*.

Page 65, 11th line of the middle paragraph, for *incapable*, read *capable*.

Page 66, 11th line of the first paragraph, for 1832, read 1830.

Page 111, bottom line, for *New*, read *New York*.

Page 114, introductory line, for *Views*, read *View*.

CONTENTS.

EDWARD D. BAKER,

THE

ORATOR AND SOLDIER.

―――――

"Whene'er he speaks, see! how the listening throng
  Dwell on the magic of his tongue,
  And when the power of eloquence he'd try,
  Here lightning strikes you, there soft breezes sigh."

PLUTARCH, that great literary ornament of his age
and country, has said: "Eloquence is to be looked for
only in a free State"; and, quoting Longinus, has further observed: "Liberty is the nurse of true greatness;
it animates the spirits and invigorates the hopes of
men; excites honorable emulation, and a desire of ex-
celling in every art. All other qualifications may be
found among those who are deprived of liberty, but
never did a slave become an orator; he can only become
a pompous flatterer."

These philosophic truths find an apt and forcible illustration in the history of our own country, which has
ever been famous for the number and ability of its orators. If there is any one thing of which the American

people are peculiarly fond, independent of an all-pervading spirit of gain, it is fine speaking. They have an unusually high, not to say inordinate admiration for men, blessed by nature with the divine gift of eloquence; and hence any man possessed of a reasonable share of brains and culture, if he be but endowed with a plausible address, fluent tongue and bold imagination, may safely calculate on sooner or later attaining honor, office and emoluments at the hands of his countrymen.

Looming proudly up at the head of this class of men, who, at different periods in the history of this Republic, have suddenly shot up in the political firmament, and shone for a time with all the dazzling radiance of meteors, is the honored name of him whose eventful and romantic history we now essay to write.

HIS BIRTH—PARENTAGE—EARLY LIFE.

It was a bleak morning, the 24th of February, 1811. in an humble apartment in the city of London—that great centre of the world's commerce, and time-honored seat of literature and civilization—that EDWARD DICKINSON BAKER first opened his eyes to behold the light of day, and his infant mind first took cognizance of the busy, bustling, teeming world around him. Of the precise rank and character of his family, it is difficult, at this distance of time and place, to form a determinate opinion, though he was evidently of pure Anglo-Saxon blood. His father, Edward Baker, was a man of considerable education, and possessed of literary tastes. His mother was a sister of Captain Thomas Dickinson of the British navy, an officer of distinction, who fought with great gallantry under Lord Collingwood at Trafalgar. Edward D. was the eldest of a family of five children, two of whom survive him, viz: Dr. Alfred Baker, of Pike county, Illinois, and a sister named Elizabeth, who married Mr. Theodore Jerome, and subsequently removed to California.

About the close of our last war with Great Britain, when Edward D. was in the fourth year of his age, his father emigrated with his family to America. Landing at Philadelphia, he engaged in the vocation of teaching, but with what success is not ascertained. Young Edward spent the ensuing ten years of his life in the city of "Brotherly Love," where some of his more distant relatives still reside, and where his name is held in affectionate remembrance.

Of his early habits and favorite pursuits, but little is known; though it appears that while a boy he was full of spirit and fire, quick of apprehension, naturally inclined to bold attempts, and likely to make a figure in the world. We are told that, in consequence of the indigence of his parents, as soon as he was old enough to engage in manual labor, he was apprenticed to a weaver, and kept at this humble and laborious trade for some years.

In 1825, the elder Baker, impelled by that restless spirit of adventure which afterwards formed so predominant a trait in the character of his gifted son, gathered together his little stock of household goods, and again turned his face westward, with the hope of improving his fortune. He first rested at the little

town of New Harmony, Indiana, in the rich valley of
the Wabash. Remaining there only a year or two, he
journeyed still further west, finally locating in Belleville, St. Clair county, Illinois, whither his son Edward
had already preceded him on foot from the Wabash.
Here he opened a select school, which he conducted
successfully for several years. Belleville, at this period,
was the most important town in the State—the home
of many of her leading men, and distinguished for the
wealth, refinement and hospitality of its inhabitants.
It was in the refined social atmosphere of this goodly
place that young Baker, then a sprightly lad of fifteen,
passed the next two or three years of his life, and his
intellect began to expand into full power and maturity.

He, perhaps, never had any taste for, if he ever
enjoyed the opportunity of pursuing, a systematic
course of study, such as has ever been considered, by
the best educators of youth, essential to the harmonious development and proper discipline of all the intellectual faculties. But he early manifested a strong
passion for books, reading with avidity everything on
which he could lay his hands, particularly History,
Biography and Poetry. It is said that his marked taste
for literature attracted the attention of the accomplished
and lamented Governor Edwards, then a resident of
Belleville, who gave the youthful student free access to
his extensive and well selected library. Possessing a
rare aptitude for acquiring information, a ready and
highly retentive memory, his mind soon became stored
with the rich treasures of literary lore, from which, in after years he drew copiously as from a perennial fountain.

From Belleville, Baker went to St. Louis in quest of employment; and here, to meet necessary expenses, he drove a dray for at least one season.

HE STUDIES LAW—MARRIES—JOINS THE CHURCH.

Dissatisfied with St. Louis, we next find him at Carrollton, the seat of justice of Greene county, Illinois, where he began the study of law in the office of Judge Caverly, serving, at the same time, as a deputy in the county clerk's office. How long he thus pursued his legal studies is undetermined; perhaps not more than a year, for as soon as he had gained a superficial knowledge of the science, being spurred on by necessity, he procured a license and commenced practice. Owing, however, to his youth, limited legal attainments, and the absence of influential friends, he met, during the first years of his professional life, with but indifferent success.

Having become entangled with an affair of the heart, Mr. Baker was married on the 27th of April, 1831, to Mrs. Mary A. Lee, a widow lady with two children, and considerably his senior in years. This alliance proved a happy one, though it added comparatively little to his fortune. Four children were born of this union—two sons and two daughters. The daughters have long since married, and with their aged and widowed mother now reside on the far Pacific coast.

Soon after his marriage, Baker joined the Reformed or Christian church, of which his wife was a worthy member. Being naturally of an impulsive and enthusiastic temperament, he was, for a time, prompt and zealous in the discharge of his religious duties, became an able exhorter, and began to entertain serious thoughts of entering upon the work of the ministry. But as years glided by, his mind becoming occupied with politics, and feverish with the gnawings of ambition, he gradually "slipped the anchor of faith," and was no longer seen in his accustomed place in the house of devotion.

It was while an active member of the Christian church that he first discovered that boldness of thought and opulence of expression, that graceful and persuasive manner of speaking, for which he became so justly celebrated in maturer life.

SERVES IN THE BLACK HAWK WAR—REMOVES TO SPRINGFIELD.

In the spring of 1832, Mr. Baker enlisted as a private in the memorable Black Hawk war, and thus improved the opportunity afforded of gratifying his early predilection for martial pursuits. He served in the volunteer ranks until the close of the campaign by the decisive battle of Broad Axe River; but it does not appear that he achieved any special distinction. In this connection, however, a story is told which will serve to illustrate his youthful daring and intrepidity. When his regiment was mustered out of service, near Dixon, on the upper waters of the Mississippi, instead of returning home overland with his comrades-in-arms, he procured a canoe from some friendly Indian, and, accompanied by a single companion, boldly descended the Father of Waters a distance of about 300 miles, to some convenient point in Calhoun county, where he landed his frail bark, and thence proceeded on foot to his home in Carrollton.

In 1835 Mr. Baker removed to Springfield, then a thriving shire town of 1500 souls. At this time he was in the 25th year of his age, and in appearance not remarkably prepossessing. His dress comported well with the straitened state of his finances. He wore a dilapidated hat of an antique pattern, and a suit of homespun jeans, loosely and carelessly thrown about him. The pants, being some inches too short, exposed to view a pair of coarse woolen socks, whilst his pedal appendages were encased in broad, heavy brogans, such as were commonly worn by the stalwart backwoodsmen of the day. Nevertheless, his step was elastic, his figure neat and trim, and the features of his face regular and pleasing to the eye. One glance at his manly countenance was sufficient to impress the observer with the belief that upon that brow " intellect sat enthroned," whilst his eyes beamed with wit and good nature. He was then as a diamond in the rough, which only needed to undergo the refining process of the lapidary, in order that its native hues might shine forth in all their original lustre.

Shortly after coming to Springfield, Mr. Baker associated himself in the practice of law with Josephus Hewitt, Esq., who afterwards removed to Natchez, Mississippi. Subsequently, he entered into partnership with the now venerable Judge Stephen T. Logan, and for a short time with Albert T. Bledsoe, late assistant Secretary of War of the late Southern Confederacy. It was here that Baker first applied himself seriously to

the duties of his profession, and here he won his first
laurels as an advocate. No town of equal size in the
West could boast of such a phalanx of forensic and
political talent as was, about this time, to be found at
the Springfield bar.

> " Here have aris'n men of towering mind,
> The praise of nations, glory of our kind.
> Those who have poured the forceful legal strain,
> Or held the assembly bound with magic strain ;
> On battle fields have shed their generous blood,
> Or midst the proudest in the council stood."

Lincoln, Douglas, McDougall, Shields, Logan, Trumbull, Stuart, McClernand, and others, were men whose
abilities, learning and eloquence would have graced any
court and dignified any bar—men who have shed unfading lustre, not alone upon the State of Illinois, but
upon the whole Union. Some of these are dead, but
others are living still, noble examples of the preceding
generation.

With such formidable rivals as these, Baker was compelled to struggle for that eminence in his profession
which he rapidly attained. Although disinclined to
close, continued study, and often negligent in the prepa-
ration of his cases, he had sufficiently mastered the
principles and intricacies of legal science as to meet the
ordinary requirements of practice, and his native genius
supplied any deficiency. His confident, self-possessed
air amidst the bustle of a court of law, his quickness
of perception, ready wit, fertility in resources, and
ardent eloquence, enabled him to achieve the victory in
spite of the most determined opposition from older or

more experienced antagonists. In jury cases he was especially successful; for in these he was less fettered by those legal forms and technicalities which ordinarily curb the reins of youthful imagination, and crush the flowers of fancy. Indeed, a jury to him was but a miniature popular assembly, before which he would pour out his argument and invective at will, or indulge in those exquisite touches of pathos, which failed not to awaken the sympathy and move the hearts of his auditors.

LAYING THE CORNER STONE OF THE OLD STATE CAPITOL.

Mr. Baker first came into public notice by being selected to deliver the oration on the occasion of laying the corner stone of the old State House in Springfield, on the 4th of July, 1837. The following concise, yet historically interesting, account of the ceremony is taken from the files of the "Sangamo Journal," under date of July 8th of that year:

"This day (July 4th) was celebrated in Springfield with unusual *eclat*. The military companies of the town, and Capt. Neale's newly organized company of horse, under the command of Major Baker, were early on parade. A *feu de joie* was fired at sunrise. After various evolutions of the military in the forenoon, they partook of a dinner furnished by Mr. W. Watson. In the afternoon a procession was formed, at the First Presbyterian church, of members of the Mechanics' Institute, with banners displayed, and citizens, who were escorted to the Methodist church by the military, where Mr. Wiley delivered a very appropriate address; after which the procession was again formed and moved to the Public Square. The imposing ceremony of laying the corner stone of the new State House was then performed. The committee for that purpose were:

"A. G. Henry, Acting Commissioner; J. F. Rague, President of Mechanics' Institute; B. Ferguson, Vice President, do.; Abner Bennett, Secretary do.; Capt. G. Elkin, Sharpshooters; J. S. Roberts, do.; J. N. Francis, do.; Capt. E. S. Phillips, of Artillery; Lieut. Wm. M. Cowgill, do.; F. C. Thornton, do.

"There were deposited in the stone a list of the chief officers of the State; a copy of the law locating the seat of government at Springfield; a copy of the journals of the last session of the General Assembly; several specimens of coins, comprising some of the late issues from the mint, as also some of the year 1795; the name of the architect, with those of the commissioners under whose superintendence the same is to be erected.

"The corner stone having been deposited in the designated place, Major Baker ascended it, and gave a short, but pertinent and animated address to the concourse of people who were present. He alluded to the occasion and the place on which we had met; glanced at the history of our State and nation: anticipated the brilliant destiny of Illinois under the controling influence of virtue and intelligence, and sought to impress on the people, that, under this influence, they might expect all they could desire for our country in the years yet to come—

> "If with the firm resolve to wear no chain,
> They dare all peril, and endure all pain;
> If their free spirits spurn a chain of gold,
> By wealth unfettered, and to ease unsold;
> If, with eternal vigilance, they tread
> In the true paths of their time-honored dead—
> Long as the star shall deck the brow of night;
> Long as the smile of woman shall be bright;
> Long as the foam shall gather where the roar
> Of ocean sounds upon the wave-worn shore—
> So long, my country, shall thy banner fly,
> Till years shall cease, and time itself shall die.*

---

* The lines here recited by Baker, formed the conclusion of a New Year's Address, written by him for the Sangamo Journal in the preceding year—1836.

"At the close of this spirited address, the welkin rang with huzzas, a salute was fired, and the people and military retired, highly gratified with the proceedings of the day."

MR. BAKER IN THE LEGISLATURE.

Enterprising and ambitious, Mr. Baker early directed his attention to politics, as opening the shortest road to preferment. In 1837, he was elected to the General Assembly from the county of Sangamon, to fill a vacancy occasioned by the resignation of Hon. Daniel Stone. In the following year he was re-elected, serving with credit on the judiciary and other committees.

When any measure of moment was to be discussed, he was generally ready with a speech; and his reputation as an orator was such, even then, that he seldom failed to secure an attentive and delighted audience; but the dry details and monotonous routine of legislative proceedings proved irksome to his impatient spirit. Hence his seat was not unfrequently vacant, and he more pleasantly, if not more profitably employed elsewhere.

During the session of 1839--40, a memorial was presented in the House of Representatives, preferring grave charges against Hon. John Pearson, Judge of the 7th judicial circuit of Illinois, and praying for his impeachment and removal from office. In due time a resolution was offered, providing for his impeachment. The subject soon assumed a partisan character, and was warmly debated—the Whigs generally favoring, and the Democrats opposing the measure. At length the House, by a party vote, decided against the impeachment.

As an embodiment of Mr. Baker's views respecting this decision of the House, and of the importance of preserving unblemished the purity of the judicial ermine, we give place to the subjoined able and earnest Protest drawn up by himself, and signed by a minority of the members, including Abraham Lincoln, one of his colleagues:

"The undersigned, members of the House of Representatives, have seen with unalloyed regret the decision of the House, in favor of the resolution against impeaching John Pearson, Judge of the 7th judicial circuit, upon the charges and specifications lately preferred against him.

"Those charges were of a high and grave character, and as evidence that they were so considered by the House, it will be seen that the House resolved, by a large majority, to have the proof relied on to sustain them. That proof has been heard; it has not only tended to sustain, but it has established, by the highest grade of testimony, every specification alleged against the respondent. Nor is there one fact stated in those specifications which has not been proved, either by the records of the Circuit court, or the oaths of two intelligent and respectable witnesses; and we have embodied in this protest some of the facts thus established. It has been proved that John Pearson, Judge of the 7th judicial circuit, has violated the right of trial by jury, by refusing the counsel for the prisoner a peremptory challenge to a juror—his prescribed number of challenges not being exhausted—alleging, as a reason therefor, a rule of practice of his circuit which was unreasonable, against the forms of law, and the letter and spirit of the Constitution. He has prevented an appeal from his decision to a higher tribunal, by refusing, in numerous cases, to sign "bills of exceptions" containing a statement of his decision, and the testimony on which such decision was based, when he, as well as the counsel in whose favor he decided, admitted these statements to be true; and when the statutes of the State, expressly making it his duty to sign such bills of exception, have been read to him, he still persisted in his refusal, saying that such statutes were but a "legislative flourish."

"He has arrogated to himself the right of final decision, subject to no appeal, by refusing to hear, and disobeying the process of the Supreme Court of the State of Illinois, commanding him to sign bills of exceptions, thereby treating the mandates of a Supreme Court with contempt, and denying an appeal from the tribunal over which he presided. He has treated with contempt and scorn the process of a Court of the United States, which he was bound to obey, by refusing to hear it, and by treating it with utter neglect. He acted in an arbitrary and oppressive manner, by threatening counsel for presenting in a respectful manner the process of the Supreme and of the District Court of the United States, and by actually punishing them for so doing, not once only, but repeatedly, under the influence of passion and excitement, thereby perverting the power placed as a sacred trust in his hands to the indulgence of personal feeling and private resentment.

"He has shown culpable ignorance of the law, by quashing an indictment for the sole reason that the clerk had left out one word in the copy delivered to the prisoner, and by quashing indictments at one term, for the single reason that the date in the caption was in figures, when the statutes of the State expressly directs the caption to be so written, thereby permitting crime to have a free course, obstructing public justice, and degrading the character of the Judiciary in the eyes of the world.

"These facts have been proved in the presence of this House, and every candid observer will bear us witness that they have received no darker coloring from our statements; and yet, with these startling facts fresh in the recollection of the House, it has been solemnly decided by a majority, in which was included every member agreeing in political sentiments with the respondent, that they did not afford reason that the said John Pearson should be impeached. That decision is final; he is again to ascend the bench; again to be entrusted with the issues of life and death, and again to officiate, not merely as a minister of stern and impartial justice, but as the representative of the majesty and dignity of the law.

"To permit this result without the formality of a trial, is, in our estimation, dangerous, if not fatal, to the purity of the judicial character. We have ever struggled to maintain the independence of the Judiciary, and to place it high above the assaults of party violence and political feeling; but we have also desired to see all Judges amenable to the law they are called upon to administer, and subject to those restraints wisely provided for in other countries, and in the Constitution of our own. We believe that, in this case, the authority of precedent, the usages of the past, and the dictates of the Constitution have been alike disregarded; and being firmly of the opinion that the decision of this House will tend to render our Judges irresponsible, and to bring our courts into contempt—to destroy the rights of individuals, and cast disrespect on the administration of public justice.

"We, therefore, present this remonstrance against the judgment of this House; and if, as citizens of the State, rejoicing in her honor and sorrowing in her shame, we shall find these predictions fulfilled, and be compelled to look back at the action of this honorable House as the fruitful source of judicial tyranny and oppression, casting a stain upon the public character, and bringing ruin to individual interest, we at least desire that all men may know that we have not assented to the decision, so we are not answerable for the consequences. Therefore, against the resolution of this House, declaring that the Hon. John Pearson, Judge, &c., should not be impeached and brought to trial, we do most respectfully but earnestly protest."

In 1840, Mr. Baker entered with ardor into the celebrated "Log Cabin" and "Hard Cider Campaign." In connection with Lincoln, Hardin and other prominent Whigs of central Illinois, he took the stump, and threw all his influence in favor of the "Tippecanoe and Tyler too" candidates of the Whig party, and against Martin

Van Buren, the Democratic candidate for President, General Harrison was triumphantly elected; but Illinois, being strongly Democratic, was carried for Mr. Van Buren by a small majority.

In the same year, Baker was elected to a seat in the Illinois State senate, which position he held for four years. Though still a young man, his abilities and experience placed him at once in the front rank, and caused him to be recognized as one of the leaders on the Whig side of the senate. He participated in every important debate—"more," perhaps as was once observed of Sir William Pulteney, "for his own improvement, than with any expectation of materially changing the vote."

HIS ELECTION TO CONGRESS.

Mr. Baker had now served with much credit and acceptability in both branches of the General Assembly. The good fortune which had thus far attended his political career, inspired him with fresh confidence in his own powers, and stimulated his ambition to reach a higher and more extended field of usefulness than that afforded by a mere State Legislature. Accordingly, in 1844, he sought and obtained the nomination for Congress in the Capital district of Illinois. Defeating his Democratic competitor, John Calhoun, (subsequently of Kansas notoriety) by a majority of 700 votes, he took his seat at Washington in December, 1845—being the only Whig representative from his State. His colleagues in this Congress were Stephen A. Douglas, John A.

McClernand, John Wentworth, Orlando B. Ficklin,
Robert Smith, and Joseph B. Hoge.

At this time the principal topic of discussion in legislative and diplomatic circles was the "Oregon Boundary" dispute, which, it was thought, would eventuate
in a war with Great Britain. Baker, ever jealous of
the honor of his adopted country, took high ground in
favor of the retention, by the United States of all territory to which claim had been laid, and was classed
among what were known as the "Fifty-four Forties, or
fight." On January 16th, 1846, he offered in the House,
the following spirited resolution expressive of his views
on this exciting question:

Resolved, That, in the opinion of this House, the President of the
United States cannot consistently, with a just regard for the honor of
the nation, offer to surrender to any foreign power any territory to
which, in his opinion, we have a clear and unquestionable title."

BRILLIANT SPEECH ON THE OREGON QUESTION.

A few days thereafter, when the resolution from the
committee on Foreign Affairs, requesting the President
to notify Great Britain of the intention of the United
States to terminate the joint occupation of Oregon, and
to abrogate the convention of 1827, was under consideration in Committee of the Whole, Mr. Baker addressed
the Committee in a speech of great eloquence and ability. favoring the adoption of the resolution. This speech
was delivered with uncommon animation, and with such
astonishing rapidity that, it is said, the reporter found
it impossible to take it down as fast as it was uttered.

In the course of his remarks, when referring to the power and greatness of his NATIVE land, he thus sublimely spoke:

"Mr. Chairman, I admit the *power* of England; it is a moral as well as a physical supremacy. It is not merely her fleets and her armies; it is not merely her colonies and her fortresses—it is more than these. There is a power in her history which compels our admiration and excites our wonder. It presents to us the field of Agincourt, the glory of Blenheim, the fortitude of "fatal Fontenoy," and the fortunes of Waterloo. It reminds us how she ruled the empire of the wave, from the destruction of the Armada to the glories of Trafalgar. Nor is her glory confined to arms alone. In arts, in science, in literature, in credit, and in commerce, she sits superior. Hers are the princes of the mind. She gives laws to learning and limits to taste. The watch-fires of her battle fields yet flash warning and defiance to her enemies, and her dead heroes and statesmen stand as sentinels upon immortal hights, to guard the glory of the living.

"Sir, it is thus I view the policy of Great Britain. I am, therefore, not concerned at the description given of it by the gentleman from South Carolina. But I confess, sir, that this conviction of her greatness makes a very different impression on his mind and on mine. He recounts her fleets, her armies, her steam marine, her colonies, as reasons for what I understand to be submission. He draws a picture of our commerce destroyed, our flag dishonored, and our sailors imprisoned; our lakes possessed by the enemy, and, worse than all, our industry destroyed, and the spirit of our people broken. Sir, what is this but an appeal to our fears? It is an appeal which will find no echo in the depths of the American heart. I, on the contrary, point to the glory of England in a spirit of emulation. She has attained her greatness by her fortitude and valor, as well as by her wisdom. She has not faltered, and, therefore, has not failed. If she has sometimes been grasping and arrogant, she has, at least, not "blenched when the storm was highest." It is true that she has steadily pursued the line of a great policy; and for that policy she has dared much and done more. She has considered her honor and her

3

essential interests as identical, and she has been able to maintain them. Sir, I would profit by her example. I would not desire to set upon light and trivial grounds. I would be careful about committing the national honor upon slight controversies. But when we have made a deliberate claim in the eyes of the world; when we persist that it is clear and unquestioned; when compromise has been offered and refused; when territory on the American continent is at stake; and when our opponent does not even claim title in herself, I would poise myself upon the magnanimity of the nation, and abide the issue."

Discussing the general policy of England, and the probabilities of a war with her, he continued:

"And if war should grow out of this Oregon question, it will not be a little war, but neither will it be a hasty one. It is not upon a sudden impulse that the peace of the world will be broken; nor will England adopt a course which has been left for the excited imagination of the gentleman to suggest.

"It appears to me, Mr. Chairman, that England will not abandon what I think to be her generally wise and statesmanlike course, for this disputed and barren territory. Unlike us, she has neither honor nor essential interests involved in the question. She has asserted no title in herself. She is only contending for the privilege of colonizing; and I do not believe that any good reason can be given why she should risk a war with us. England will, no doubt, see that she has much to lose, and nothing to gain. I repeat, sir, I do not think that our assertion of our right to the whole territory ought to lead to war.

"But, Mr. Chairman, suppose it to be otherwise; how does the argument stand then? We assert this territory to be ours. The President believes it, our negotiator believes it, this House believes it, the country believes it. But, say gentlemen, "England will go to war." In my opinion this will not be so; but if she does, is that a reason for surrendering our rights? If it be, national honor is dead within us. I know that whenever a western man touches upon this view of the subject, it renders him liable to a sneer at what gentlemen are pleased to call "western enthusiasm." I desire to treat this as an American question, and I shall not be driven from that course. I am not one of those who supported Mr. Polk. I used the utmost of my ability to prevent his election; and when Mr. Clay was beaten, I confess, I felt as the friends of Aristides may be supposed to have felt when he was driven from Athens. I had no share in the Democratic Baltimore Convention. I thought then, and think now, that it was unwise and unfair to attempt to make "Oregon" a party watchword. And I believe that much of the difficulty in which we now find ourselves arises from that course. But when the question is made—when our title is asserted—when the opinions of our people, based, perhaps, upon the action of Congress, have become fixed, and we are willing to maintain our rights at any sacrifice, then many of the movers of this agitation begin to falter. Some have got Texas and are content—some have become enamored of "white robed peace"—some clamor for 49 deg. and compromise—but they all join in deprecating "western enthusiasm." Sir, the West will be true to its convictions. I believe that portion of the West which sustained Mr. Polk will still be for the whole of Oregon. And, sir, I think that those who opposed him, many of whom believed the Democratic outburst for Oregon to be a mere party maneuver, will now consider it an American question, and stand by the country. Such, sir, will be my course on this floor.

Speaking in defense of the restless, pioneering spirit of Western men, he said:

"There was another remark made in the course of this debate, which may merit a reply. It was said that it was the restless spirit of Western men which caused this trouble by their occupation of Oregon, and they were ridiculed for seeking homes across the Rocky Mountains. I desire gentlemen to remember that it has been the policy of this Government to encourage the settlement of the West. Our whole system of land laws, and especially our pre-emption laws, have had that tendency. And as to Oregon itself, this House has received with the greatest favor, for several preceding sessions, a bill for the express purpose of encouraging settlement on the borders of the Pacific. Sir, it is to the spirit which prompts these settlers that we are indebted for the settlement of the Western States. The men who are going to beat down roads and level mountains—to brave and overcome the terrors of the wilderness—are our brethren and our kinsmen. It is a bold and free spirit; it has in it the elements of grandeur. They will march, not

> Like some poor exile, bending with his woe,
> To stop too fearful, and too faint to go;

But they will go with free steps; they will bear with them all the arts of civilization, and they will found a Western Empire. Sir, it is possible they may not receive protection, but, at least, they should be shielded from reproach.

In concluding this able and statesman-like effort, Mr. Baker discussed the "Monroe doctrine" at some length. showing its bearing upon the question at issue; and indulged in a prophetic view of the future destiny of our country:

"I suppose, sir," said he, "that when Mr. Monroe made his famous declaration of 1823, he designed it to have some practical application. That portion of it referring to European interference with South American politics was occasioned by the attempt of the Holy Alliance to assist the Bourbons to recover an ascendency in South America. But that portion of it which denied that 'any unsettled portion of the continent was the subject for future European colonization,' was intended to apply to the north west coast of the Pacific, the very territory in question. It was so treated in the debate on the Panama mission, and Judge White, of Tennessee, expressly so stated in that discussion. A moment's reflection will make it apparent that this was its object; it was indeed the only considerable territory to which it could refer. I don't consider, sir, that when a declaration of this general character is made by a President or Congress, that we are bound to sustain it by force of arms whenever its principles are violated. But I insist that it was a statement of a great American policy; that it well became our growing importance; that subsequent events—our increase in population, in States, in commerce, in all that constitutes greatness—will give it still greater authority. And I submit that this is the very case which demands its practical application. This territory is unsettled; it is on this continent; it is contiguous to this Union. As long as it was merely ground for hunting and trapping, and trade with Indians, it was of but little consequence. But now the wave of population breaks across the peaks of the Rocky Mountains, and mingles its spray with the Pacific. It is becoming settled, and will soon be of commercial importance. The question is, shall we permit it to remain open to foreign colonization? I say that question should be determined, judging of us not merely as we are, but as we probably shall be.

"The doctrine that a nation has a right to regard the preservation of its vital interests, in such a controversy, is to be found in the best considered papers of modern times. It is the province of enlightened statemanship to look forward, and no statesman can fail to perceive the importance of that territory to this Union. To divide the country would be to build up rival and conflicting interests—to permit England to build up a commercial if not a military Gibralter on the Pacific coast. It would be to surrender all chance of fair and equal rivalry in commercial enterprise in that sea. It would be to put England in possession of another key to control what may be the seat of a vast commerce. Mr. Chairman, I think that to abandon the principles of Mr. Monroe's declaration would be to falter in the path which providence has marked out for us, and to prove ourselves unworthy of a high destiny. It is not thus that England has 'halted by the wayside.' She has gone onward with a steady and imperial march. She has seen her destiny, and has pursued it; and she has made a small island on the borders of Europe the seat of the mightiest power the world has ever known. The seat of our power is a vast continent. We are widely separated from Europe, and unconnected with its politics. In the very spring and vigor of our youth, we too, are pressing onward with the steps of a giant. Ours will be the predominating power on this continent; and our permanent peace and our essential interests will be jeopardized by any foreign colonization.

"Would Great Britain permit us to colonize any portion of India contiguous to her possessions? Would she permit us to annex any dependent state, if there was one, on her East India frontier? Would we permit her to conquer or purchase Cuba? No sir. It is in this sense I would apply the doctrine of ' manifest destiny,' so often remarked in debate. It is an expression which I did not originate, and which does not convey my idea ; but, sir, I would not be willing to shut my eyes to the argument contained in the phrase itself. The doctrine of natural boundaries sometimes establishes a title to a country. A deep river, a rolling ocean, an unsettled country, a contiguous territory— all lend force to our pretentions. Providence has separated us from the Old World ; and our policy as well as our institutions should perpetuate the division.

" In conclusion, it only remains for me to say that I am as far, as any gentleman on this floor, from a desire to precipitate this country and Great Britian into a war. I believe that peace is the policy of both countries. We are running a career of earnest (I trust not ungenerous) rivalry, and we are both disseminating the English language, the principles of free government, and the blessings of religious toleration. Yet I believe that this *notice* is the best mode of maintaining peace, if it can be maintained on honorable terms ; but if we can only preserve peace by a surrender of American territory ; by adopting a course as impolitic as it would be degrading, I shall give my vote for every measure the honor of the country may demand, under what, I trust, is a true sense of my responsibility as a legislator and a man."

The ardent support which Mr. Baker lent to the administration of President Polk on the Oregon question, seems to have drawn upon him the censure of some of his more bigoted Whig associates. He, therefore, availed himself of the first favorable opportunity to rise in the House, to a personal explanation, and defined his position in the following characteristic style:

He said : "I was opposed to his (Polk's) election. I am opposed to every measure of his administraton of a mere party character. I need not say this in my own district, or to my own people, but I desire to say it here, so that wherever the report shall go, the correction may go also—wherever the bane goes, the antidote may follow. I now say that, except so far as Mr. Polk may be for the honor of our country in our foreign relations, I am opposed to him. I rejoice in being a Whig. I would rather be a Whig defeated, than a Democrat successful. I am for Mr. Clay. I would be willing to run him again. I had rather vote for him than any man in the world, and I take this occasion to say, that, as in all times past I have given my warm support to Whig men, and Whig principles; so in either fortune, amid disaster and defeat, to the very last of my blood and breath, I am a Whig, constant and unchanging, now and forever."

MR. BAKER'S LETTER TO HIS CONSTITUENTS—HE LECTURES IN BALTIMORE.

In the latter part of February, 1846, Mr. Baker addressed a lengthy letter to the people of the 7th Congressional district of Illinois, on the subject of the English Corn Laws, and the influence their repeal was likely to exert upon the agricultural interests of this country. This letter, disclosing on the part of the writer, an intimate acquaintance with the laws of political economy, attracted considerable attention, and attained a wide circulation through the press.

Notwithstanding his many public duties and engagements, Baker, about this time, found leisure to deliver an elaborate lecture, in Baltimore, on the subject of the " Influence of Commerce upon Civilization." The following interesting synopsis of this lecture is taken from the " Baltimore American" of that date:

" The 5th lecture of the course, in aid of the Sabbath School attached to the Rev. Mr. Hanmer's church, was pronounced last evening by the Hon. E. D. Baker, member of Congress from Illinois, to a large and highly appreciative audience. The influence of commerce upon civilization, formed the basis of his discourse. It afforded a wide and fertile field for intellectual research ; and we are pleased to say.that, the lecturer travelled over and explored it most satisfactorily. He evinced a studious, patient investigation of, and thorough acquaintance with the world's history. The march of civilization had been onward, hand in hand with the encouragement and spread of commerce. Its neglect for the accomplishment of mere military renown, had been in all ages, and was destined to be, followed by a deterioration of general happiness, and nobler virtues of the human race. This, part of the early history of Greece and Rome, and other places, renowned in ancient times for their elevation to greatness, and subsequent prostration, fully attested. With the establishment of commercial intercourse between nations, was introduced, of necessity, the refinements and virtues of civilized life. They became a part of the traffic. Whilst one people invited to their ports the merchandise of another, if they were more advanced in mental accomplishments, those who come amongst them were made partakers of their superior advantages, and exchanged not only commodities of physical traffic, but obtained from association incitements to refinement, and were induced to imitate the example of their superior in moral excellence. In like manner, when the more civilized nations of the earth pushed their commerce into other portions of the globe, they carried with them characteristic virtues—the advantages of which were seen, admired and imitated.

"As the world grew older and its population increased, both sea and land, from the smallest to the most extended scale, became a grand theatre of commercial enterprise ; changing and interchanging commodities of traffic, as well as the principles of civilization. The views of the speaker upon this point were beautiful, eloquent, and comprehensive. He left no room to doubt that the influence of commerce upon civilization was all-powerful. It carried the most ingenious arts, and approved sciences into the very midnight of human habitations; the seeds of which being sown, soon sprung up, fertilizing and ameliorating the condition of man—producing abundant harvest, which, in the fullness of time, was gathered in to nourish the great cause of moral excellence and progressive civilization.

"The lecture, throughout, was heard by an attentive and admiring audience; who were not only agreeably entertained, but, we feel confident, received there from information highly beneficial. The Speaker's manner of delivery was accomplished, and the style and language of his lecture, choice and elegant. The closing portion was truly beautiful, charming the hearer in enraptured admiration."

HE TAKES PART IN THE MEXICAN WAR—SPEECH ON THAT SUBJECT.

When the war broke out with Mexico, Baker's martial spirit was fully aroused. Having, as we have already mentioned, seen some service in one of our frontier wars with the Indians, he could not now content himself to luxuriate in inglorious ease, whilst others were winning laurals on the "tented field." He accordingly hastened home to raise a regiment of volunteers, and proceed to the theatre of strife, where battles were to be fought and glory won.

"The announcement of his name and purpose was as magical as the summons of Rhoderic Dhu; more offered than could be accepted—

"From the gray sire, whose trembling hand
   Could hardly buckle on his band,
To the raw boy, whose shaft and bow
   Were yet scarce terror to the crow,
Till at the rendezvous they stood,
   By hundreds prompt for blows or blood."

His regiment being promptly filled, it was accepted by the Government, as the 4th Illinois Infantry. On arriving at Matamoras, on the Rio Grande, he soon discovered that the troops stood greatly in need of additional tent equipage, munitions of war, &c. Remaining in camp for a few months, he accepted the position of a bearer of despatches to the War Department, and repaired to Washington. Congress being in session, and not having resigned his seat in the House, he availed himself of his privilege as a member to make a speech of magical power, in favor of a vigorous prosecution of the war, and in behalf of the volunteers then in the field—whose wants, he contended, it was the duty of the government at once to supply.

We present here a few leading extracts from this fine impromptu effort, delivered December 28th, 1846. Mr. Baker began as follows:

"Mr. Speaker, I desire to return my sincere acknowledgments to those gentlemen on both sides of the House, who, I know, have been anxious to obtain the floor, but have kindly yielded it to me that I might have the opportunity of addressing to the House a few hasty remarks, before returning to the army in Mexico. While I thank the gentlemen for this act of courtesy, I beg leave to say that I understand it to be intended by them as a tribute to the gallantry and devotion of the brave men with whom I am associated. For myself, I must say, that I feel humbled when I remember how little I have done to deserve such kindness, or to entitle me to any such mark of regard. I could wish it had been the fortune of the gallant Davis—formerly a member on this floor, but now far distant, engaged in fighting for his country— to now stand where I do, and to receive from gentlemen on all sides the congratulations so justly due to him, and to listen to the praises of his brave compeers. For myself, I have been unfortunately left far in the rear of the war, and, if now, I venture to say a word in behalf of those who have endured the severest hardships of the struggle, whether in the bloody streets of Monterey, or in a yet sterner form on the banks of the Rio Grande, I beg gentlemen to believe that while I feel this a most pleasant duty, it was with others a duty full of pain; for I stand here, after six months service as a volunteer, having seen no actual warfare in the field.

"It is not without profound astonishment that I have observed the course of the present debate, as it has thus far proceeded. I am sure that it was not imagined, and would scarce be believed by my brave companions in Mexico, that in this the third week of the session, the American Congress was in grave debate on the subject of mobs in Ohio, and by what numerical majorities certain individuals have been chosen to the next Congress. The men who have fought at Palo Alto, at Resaca and at Monterey had not expected this. The men who have endured on the banks of the Rio Grande all that fierce disease, aggravated by the want of even the necessaries, whether of war or of mere subsistance; half clothed, hardly fed, are looking from Matamoras and Tampico, with all the earnestness of their souls for the moment of advance; whose eyes are looking for aid, support and encouragement from Congress, and their friends at home—these men certainly have not anticipated such a spectacle on this floor as I have had the pain to witness, and must suffer the still greater pain of declaring to them.

"I am constrained by what I have seen and heard to believe that Congress is not quite informed as to the actual state of things in Mexico. However this may be, I have a few facts to state, to which I respectfully invite your attention. It is not my purpose to engage for a moment in anything like political or party controversy. Where my sympathies have once been, I need not state; and where they have been, there they still are, and there they will remain through good and through evil fortune, unchanged. But at present, I cannot perceive that the question of Whig or Democrat has to be put in order to decide upon the only question which is now, or ought to be, before the House; and my object is to urge the members of the House, without regard to party difference, to act immediately, to act efficiently in behalf of the gallant army, now toiling, bleeding and suffering in a foreign land.

" In the first place, the army in Mexico needs more men, and more money ; and they need it now, without delay. I have been informed that the entire force now in the field, including Taylor's column, Butler's division, Wool's column, and Patterson's division, is not over 11,500 men, excluding perhaps Gates' artillery battalion, and two other regiments, now recruiting, and some troops which may have arrived by this time at Tampico. With this amount of force, there is an area of country to be covered which it is difficult to describe. Commencing at Monterey, it extends to Saltillo, Montemoredoz, Matamoras, Camargo, Coahuila, and through Victoria to Tampico itself, and as much farther as we may be able to penetrate. Of this number, it will require at least 3,000 to garrison Saltillo and Monterey, and thus hold the advance we have already made in that direction, exclusive of Chihuahua, Santa Fe, and California ; and besides what will be necessary in order to garrison the various other posts we have established, whether for peaceful or military purposes.

"I understand that the Congress and President of the United States, kindled into ardor by the glories which are gilding the national eagles, are longing for new conquests, and panting to witness fresh triumphs of our arms. In that hope, I myself most fervently join. But I would press upon the House whether, let the army approach the city of Mexico, either by the way of Ft. St. Juan, or by that of St. Louis Potosi, it is possible with ten, or twelve, or fourteen thousand men to cover the country we have, and push our advance to the consummation of the war. I express the opinion, not without diffidence, but must say I doubt whether it is possible with that amount of the very best soldiers America ever sent into the field (and better men never were sent from any country) to conquer eight millions of people. Let it be recollectd that this little army of fifteen thousand men is scattered over an area of country extending five hundred miles from North to South, where all the mean sof communication are uncertain, and is filled with a hostile population. How can such a number of soldiers, even the best disciplined and the most skilful and experienced, divided into two or three columns, separately operating, be expected to prosecute their advance, and have it marked, as it has thus far been, only with glory and honor ?

" But it is asked, what use would it be to reinforce the army to any great extent, because even if we secure the capital itself, and plant our standard over the city of Mexico, we shall be no nearer peace than we are on this day? If that is true, it surely ought to have been considered before we commenced the war, and especially before we commenced an invasion of the Mexican territory. Mexico commenced an attack on what we claimed as American soil, and I am not one of those who were for yielding it up to them, either then or now. If the war is just, it does not follow that it is a war of invasion; as a war of defence, it has been most glorious to the American arms. So far as it can be called a war upon the ocean, we have it in our power to laugh all opposition to scorn. A war of invasion has not been necessarily incumbent upon us; yet the House voted the supplies for its prosecution almost unanimously. There was, as I understand, scarcely a dissenting voice as to the propriety of the advance of our army. All parties, and all classes of people among us, were agreed, that, if we made war at all, it ought to be sudden, vigorous, and brief. The army did advance accordingly, and we have gained in a brief space of time three great battles. We have advanced, it is true, some three hundred miles into the Mexican territory, yet we have scarcely, to any perceptible extent, weakened the country, or crippled its resources. On the contrary, it is a matter of not a little doubt, whether Mexico is not stronger this day than she has ever been; more united, more naturalized; more concentrated in one public feeling; looking more unitedly towards a single leader. From this state of things, if it does indeed exist, Congress ought to derive a deeper and more impressive sense of its duty in relation to this war, and of its duty now."

Passing to consider the attitude taken by the Whig party with reference to the war, he proceeded:

"As a Whig, do I still occupy a place on this floor; nor do I think it worth while to reply to such a charge as that the Whigs are not friends of their country, because many of them doubt the justice or expediency of the present war. Surely, there was more evidence of the patriotism of the man, who, doubting the expediency and even the entire justice of the war, nevertheless supported it, because it was the war of his country. In the one it might be mere enthusiasm, and an impetuous temperament; in the other it was true patriotism, a sense of duty. Homer represents Hector as strongly doubting the expediency of the war against Greece—gave his advice against it—had no sympathy with Paris, whom he bitterly reproached, much less with Helen; yet, when the war came, and the Grecian forces were marshalled on the plain, and their crooked keels were seen cutting the sands of the Trojan coast, Hector was a flaming fire—his beaming helmet was seen in the thickest of the fight. There are in the American army many who have the spirit of Hector; who strongly doubt the propriety of the war, and especially the manner of its commencement; who, yet, are ready to pour out their hearts' best blood like water, and their lives with it, on a foreign shore, in defence of the American flag, and American glory."

Considering the question of advance, the condition of the army and what it would accomplish, he said:

" Then there is another thing which ought to be well considered: whatever advance our forces make, must be made during the coming winter. The reasons must be obvious. Less than six months ago Congress had sent into the field as many as twenty regiments of volunteers, all burning with the most exalted hopes, and ready to peril their all, health, reputation, and even life itself—not in a defensive, but in an invasive war—not undertaken to defend their own homes and firesides, but for the glory of the American name and arms. Alas, how many of those fine young men who had never seen a battle—never had cast their stern glance on the countenance of an enemy, were now sleeping their last long sleep on the banks of the Rio Grande. Once their hearts heaved high with a soldier's fondest hopes—proud and high had been their measured footsteps, as they marched in all the buoyancy of youthful ambition, but now—

" Where rolls the rushing Rio Grande,
    How peacefully they sleep;
  They did not fall in bloody strife,
    Upon a well fought field;

Not from the red wound poured the life
  Where cowering foeman yield.
The archangel's shade was slowly cast
  Upon each polished brow,
But calm and fearless to the last
  They sleep securely now."

"The bones of nearly two thousand young men, in whose veins some of the best blood of the country flowed, are now resting in the mold, on the banks of the Rio Grande—who had never seen the face of an enemy, and who had never had the opportunity of striking one manly blow in behalf of their country and their race." * * * *

"I can pledge myself for the army that it will do its duty, its whole duty, to the country. It is burning for the advance; it pants for such another conflict as that at Monterey beneath the walls of Mexico, but at the same time it desires peace—honorable peace—a peace conquered by our arms. I believe that, if suitably sustained, the army will conquer that peace, and sign it within the palaces of Mexico within the next four months."

After making this stirring speech, for which he was highly complimented by the advocates of the war, Baker left Washington, and rejoined his regiment on the Rio Grande. Shortly thereafter, he was transferred from Gen. Taylor's to Gen. Scott's military department, and arrived in time to share in the short, yet victorious siege of Vera Cruz.

He went forward into the interior of Mexico with the main body of Gen. Scott's army, and bravely led his men to the charge under the "leaden hail" and "sheeted fire," which rained upon them from the frowning and embattled heights of Cerro Gordo. When the intrepid and chivalrous General Shields fell at the head of his brigade, badly wounded, Col. Baker immediately assumed command of the same, made a gallant charge upon the enemy's works, turned their flank, drove them from their position, and contributed materially towards winning that splendid victory which forms one of the brightest chapters in the history of the Mexican war, and an unfading laurel in General Scott's chaplet of fame.

Not long after the battle of Cerro Gordo, the term of enlistment of Col. Baker's regiment expired, and the men not desiring to re-enlist, were mustered out of service. He was, therefore, reluctantly, compelled to quit the field before the successful termination of the war.

HE REMOVES TO GALENA—IS RE-ELECTED TO CONGRESS.

Returning home, he resumed the practice of his profession. But he was too much a man of action to long remain in the secluded paths of private or professional life. Seeing no immediate prospect of political preferment in the congressional district which he had formerly represented, (Mr. Lincoln having taken his place) he removed, in the Spring of 1848, to Galena, Illinois— up into the lead-bearing region. Such was his skill and address as a politician, and such his peculiar tact for winning popular favor, that, after a residence in Galena of only about three months, he was returned to Congress from that district, by a majority over his Democratic competitor of 1,000 votes—a feat, which, at the time, perhaps, no one but Baker would have undertaken, much less successfully accomplished. But he had one of those pliable temperaments which, Proteus-like, could easily adapt itself to the tastes and temper of the people of any district in which he happened to reside; and he happened, temporarily at least, to reside in a good many.

As one of the Whig electors for the State at large, Col. Baker was also active in the Presidential campaign of 1848, advocating with characteristic zeal and energy, the claims of his old commander, Zachary Taylor. Few men were more effective on the stump, in the heat of a political canvass. The masses admired him for his talents and valor, whilst they loved him for his easy familiarity and agreeable social qualities. His speeches were clear, pointed, and eloquent presentations of his political views, abounding in happy hits and well turned periods, and always captivated the crowd. He dealt unsparingly with his opponents; and if at a loss for arguments to sustain his position, he would overwhelm them with ridicule and sarcastic wit.

Col. Baker took his seat for the second time in the federal House of Representatives in December, 1849, He bore an active, if not a conspicuous part in the debates upon those grave national issues which formed so prominent a feature in the first session of the 31st Congress, and which so profoundly agitated the country at that time. He was understood to favor some of the measures of Compromise passed by Congress during this session. Most of them, however, failed to command his approbation or support. The annexed paragraph, taken from a speech made by him on these historic questions, was prophetic of his future fate:

4

" I have only to say, that, if the time should come when disunion rules the hour, and discord reigns supreme, I shall again be ready to give the best blood in my veins to my country's cause. I shall be prepared to meet all antagonists, with lance in rest, to do battle in every land in defense of the Constitution of the country, which I have sworn to support to the last extremity, against disunionists, and all its enemies, whether North or South—to meet them everywhere, at all times, with speech or hand, with word or blow, until thought and being shall be mine no longer."

HIS EULOGIUM ON PRESIDENT TAYLOR.

During the same session of this Congress, on the 10th of July, 1850, Mr. Baker delivered a glowing and pathetic eulogy on the career and character of President Taylor, who had expired at the Executive mansion on the day previous. This unexpected and painful event cast a gloom over the entire land, and drew forth appropriate and feeling addresses from the most eminent orators of the Senate and House of Representatives. Yet for purity and beauty of diction, felicity of illustration, and accuracy in portraying the character of the illustrious deceased, Baker's panegyric was unsurpassed, if, indeed, equalled by any pronounced on the floor of either House. It is probably the finest specimen of his eloquence extant, and sparkles like a gem amongst the ordinarily dry details of the Congressional Globe. He spoke as follows:

" Mr. Speaker: It is often said of sorrow, that, like death, it levels all distinctions. The humblest heart can heave a sigh as deep as the proudest; and I avail myself of this mournful privilege to swell the accents of grief which have been poured forth to-day, with a larger though not more sincere utterence.

"A second time since the foundation of this Government, a President of the United States has been stricken by death in the performance of his duties. The blow which strikes the man, falls upon the nation's heart, and the words of saddened praise which fall on our ears to-day, and here, are but echoes of the thoughts which throng in the hearts of millions that mourn him everywhere.

" You have no doubt observed, sir, that in the first moments of a great loss, the instincts of affection prompt us to summon up the great and good qualities of those for whom we weep. It is a wise ordination of Divine Providence. A generous pride tempers and restrains the bitterness of grief, and noble deeds and heroic virtues shed a consoling light upon the tomb. It is in this spirit that I recur for an instant, and an instant only, to the events of a history fresh in in the memory of the nation, and the world. The late President of the United States has devoted his whole life to the service of his country. Of a nature singularly unambitious, he seems to have combined the utmost gentleness of manner, with the greatest firmness of purpose. For more than thirty years, the duties of his station confined him to a sphere, where only those who knew him most intimately, could perceive the qualities, which danger quickened and brightened into sublimity and grandeur.

" In the late war with Great Britain, he was but a captain; yet the little band who defended Fort Harrison, saw, amid the smoke of battle, that they were commanded by a man fit for his station. In the Florida campaign, he commanded but a brigade; yet his leadership not only evinced courage, but his conduct inspired this quality in the breast of the meanest soldier in the ranks. He begun the Mexican campaign at the head of only a division; yet as the events of the war swelled that division into an army, so the crisis kindled him into higher resolves and nobler actions, till the successive steps of advance, became the assured march of victory.

"As we review the brilliant and stirring passages of the events to which I refer, it is not in the power of sudden grief to suppress the admiration which thrills our hearts. When, sir, has there been such a campaign ? When such soldiers to be led ? and when such qualities of leadership so variously combined ? How simple, and yet how grand the announcement : 'In whatever force the enemy may be, I shall fight him.' It gave Palo-Alto, and Resaca to our banner. How steadfast the resolution that impelled the advance to Monterey ! How stirring the courage which beleaguered the frowning city ; which stormed the barricaded street ; which carried the embattled heights, and won, and kept the whole. Nor, Sir, can we forget that in the flush of victory the gentle heart stayed the bold hand, while the conquering soldier offered sacrifices on the altar of pity, amid all the exaltation of triumph.

" Sir, I may not stop to speak of the achievements of Buena Vista. They are deeds that will never die. It was the great event of the age —a contest of races, and institutions. An army of volunteers, engaged not in an impetuous advance, but in a last extremity—men, who had never seen fire, faced the foe with the steadiness of veterans. Sir, as long as those frowning heights and bloody ravines shall remain, these recollections will endure ; and with them the name of the man who steadied every rank, and kindled every eye by the indomitable resolution which would not yield, and the exalted spirit which rose highest amid the greatest perils.

" Is was from scenes like these he was called to the Chief Magistracy. It was a summons unexpected and unsought—the spontaneous expression of a noble confidence—the just reward of great actions.

" It may not be proper, here and now, to speak of the manner in which the new duties were executed; but I may say, that here, as elsewhere, he exhibited the same firmness which has marked his life. He was honest, and unostentatious ; he obeyed the law, and loved the constitution ; he dealt with difficult questions with a singleness of purpose which is the truest pilot amid storms. Nor can it be doubted that when impartial history shall record the events of his administration, they will be found worthy of his life, and a firm foundation for his future renown.

"You remember, Mr. Speaker, that when the great Athenian philosopher was inquired of by the Lydian king, as to who was the happiest among men, he declared that no man should be declared happy until his death. The President of the United States has so finished a noble life, as to justify the pride and admiration of his countrymen; he has faced the last enemy with a manly firmness, and a becoming resolution. He died, where an American citizen would most desire to die—not amid embattled hosts, and charging squadrons —but amidst weeping friends, and an anxious nation—in the house provided by its gratitude, only to be taken thence to a 'house not made with hands, eternal in the Heavens.'

"Sir, in the death which has caused so much dismay, there is a becoming resemblance to the life which has created so much confidence. His closing hours were marked with a beautiful calmness; his last expressions indicated a manly sense of his own worth, and a consciousness that he had done his duty. Nor can I omit to remark, that it is this sense of the obligations of duty, which appears to have been the true basis of his character. In boyhood, and in age; as a captain, and as a general; whether defending a fort against savages, or exercising the functions of Chief Magistrate, duty, rather than glory, self approval, rather than renown, have prompted the deeds which have made him immortal.

"The character upon which death has just set its seal, is filled with beautiful and impressive contrasts. A warrior, a man of action, he sighed for retirement. Amid the events which crowned him with fame, he counselled a withdawal of our troops. And whether at the head of armies, or in the chair of State, he appeared as utterly unconscious of his great renown, *as if no banner had drooped at his word; as if no gleam of glory had shown through his whitened hair.*

"It is related of Epaminonidas, that when fatally wounded at the battle of Mantinea, they bore him to a height, from whence, with fading glance, he surveyed the fortunes of the fight; and when the field was won laid himself down to die. The friends who had gathered around him, wept his early fall, and passionately expressed their sorrow that he had died childless. 'Not so,' said the hero with his last breath, 'for do I not leave two fair daughters, Leuctre, and Mantinea.' Gen. Taylor is more fortunate, since he leaves an excellent, and most worthy family to deplore his loss, and inherit his glory. Nor is he fortunate in this only, since, like Epaminonidas, he leaves not only two, but four battles, Palo Alto, Resaca, Monterey, and Buena Vista—the grand creations of his genius and valor, to be remembered as long as truth and courage appeal to the human heart.

"Mr. Speaker, the occasion and the scene impress upon us a deep sense of the instability of all human affairs, so beautifully alluded to by my friend from Massachusetts, (Mr. Winthrop.) The great Southern Senator is no longer among us. The President during whose administration the war commenced, 'sleeps in the house appointed for all the living,' and the great soldier who had led the advance, and assured the triumph, 'lies like a warrior taking his rest.' *Ah! sir, if in this assembly there is a man whose heart beats with tumultuous, and unrestrained ambition, let him to-day stand by the bier on which that lifeless body is laid, and learn how much of human greatness fades in an hour. But if there be another here, whose fainting heart shrinks from a noble purpose, let him too, visit those sacred remains, to be reminded how much there is in true glory that can never die.*"

THE PANAMA RAILROAD.

In the beginning of the year 1851, Colonel Baker's restless and original mind seized upon an enterprise as " wild as it was engaging." He entered into an agreement with the Panama Railroad Company, of New York, to grade a portion of that great inter-oceanic line of communication known as the Panama Railroad. Pursuant to this agreement, he collected a company of about 400 laborers, in the West, and sent them in charge of his brother, Dr. Alfred Baker, to the Isthmus of Panama. He soon thereafter sailed himself to Navy Bay, (now Aspinwall) the Atlantic terminous of the road, to superintend his work.

Here, under the vertical rays of an equator's sun, amidst the tangled forests and luxuriant vegetation of the Isthmus, with its interminable swamps, teeming with noxious insects, venomous reptiles, and reeking with deadly malaria, or beside the slimy banks of the tortuous river, Chagres, Baker and his hardy band, labored and toiled for many weary months, until most of them were either disabled from further service, or had fallen victims to the malarious fevers of the tropics. At last their gallant leader fell sick, nigh unto death; was compelled to give up his undertaking, abandon the country, and return home to recruit his shattered energies.

The building of the Panama Railroad was an enterprise of such magnitude and importance, that we have thought proper to give a brief outline of its history, before proceeding further with our narrative.

The daring project of connecting the Atlantic and Pacific oceans, by a line of railway across the Isthmus of Darien or Panama, was conceived by Mr. William H. Aspinwall, a large-minded capitalist of the city of New York, in 1848. He had already taken a contract for the establishment of a line of steamships on the Pacific, from Panama to California, to be run in connection with a similar line on the Atlantic, to New York. Having satisfied himself of the entire feasibility of the enterprise, Mr. Aspinwall, together with Mr. Henry Chauncey, and Mr. John L. Stephens, formed a contract with the Government of New Granada for the construction of the road, which was to be completed in eight years.

Up to this time, (the latter part of 1848) calculations for the ultimate success of the undertaking, were based upon the advantages it would afford in shortening by many thousand miles, not only the route to California and Oregon, but to China, Australia, and the East Indies, and in the development of the rich countries bordering the Pacific coast. The discovery of gold in California, however, with its accompanying tide of emigration across the Isthmus, changed the prospects of the projected road, and from an enterprise which looked far into the future for its rewards, it became one promising immediate returns from the capital and labor invested. A charter was now obtained from the Legislature of the State of New York, for the formation of a stock company, under which one million dollars of stock was soon taken—the original grantees having, meanwhile, transferred their contract into the hands of this company. In the early part of 1849, a large and experienced party of engineers was sent down to the Isthmus to survey and locate the line of the road. This difficult task being satisfactorily accomplished, a contract was then entered into with Messrs. George M. Totten, and John C. Trautwine for the building of the road. Subsequently, these gentlemen were released from their obligations as contractors, at their own request, but retained as engineers—the company having concluded to take charge of the construction themselves. Under the superintendence, mainly, of these bold, skilful and determined engineers, the work was commenced in May, 1850, and pushed forward with remarkable vigor, despite the most formidable obstacles, and dispiriting influences. As the work progressed, laborers were drawn from almost every quarter of the globe, great numbers of whom perished by exposure in the terrible marshes on the Atlantic slope of the Isthmus, and with the deadly fevers incident to the country. At length, after the expenditure of several million dollars, and the sacrifice of thousands of lives, the last rail of the road was laid at midnight, on the 27th of January, 1855, and, on the following day, a locomotive passed over it from ocean to ocean—a distance of fifty miles.

Thus was built and completed this great commercial highway of nations—a work which will endure for centuries, a noble monument to the memories of the men who had the genius to contrive, and the ability, courage, and perseverance to carry it to a successful termination.*

COLONEL BAKER IN CALIFORNIA.

When the bracing air of the Illinois prairies had restored Baker to something of his accustomed health and vigor, he turned his gaze eagerly towards the golden sands of the Pacific coast, whither the wave of emigration was then swiftly rolling. Heaps of untold wealth and political honors higher than any he had yet attained, rose alternately before his excited imagination, and allured him westward to the land of promise.

---

*The above account is chiefly condensed from an able article on the Panama Railroad, published in Harpers' Magazine for January, 1859.

In 1852. he emigrated with his family to California. Establishing himself in San Francisco. he once more resumed the practice of law. His fame as an advocate and orator had preceded him, so that he soon found himself in the midst of an extensive and diversified business. Almost at one bound, and apparently with but little effort, he rose to the summit of his profession, and to a share in the best practice in the courts of that youthful commercial metropolis. This position he retained with comparative ease during the period of his residence in San Francisco. Here it was that he achieved his highest reputation as a lawyer, and perhaps his most brilliant renown as an orator.

He might now be considered a prosperous man. His clients were numerous. and constantly increasing. His income was large—for he always charged good fees— and his means ample to live in a style befitting a man of prudence, taste and refinement. But all the gold of the new El Dorado would hardly have sufficed for Baker. With heedless improvidence he spent all he earned, and something more. Hence. there were times when he revelled in luxury, and other times, again, when he had scarcely a penny in his purse.

He early identified himself with the Free Soil movement in California. and became conspicuous as a leader of the party opposed to the extension of slavery. In 1855, he was a candidate of that party for the State Senate, and made a stirring canvass; but the Democracy being largely in the majority, he sustained a Waterloo defeat. In 1856. he was one of the first to unfurl the Fremont and Dayton banner on the Pacific slope, and dauntlessly led the forlorn hope of the Republicans in that spirited Presidential contest. Subsequently, he was an unsuccessful candidate for Congress. These repeated defeats, in successive campaigns, were enough to have discouraged and deterred an ordinary politician. But with Baker they were simply incidents of the day, and served rather to inspire him to renewed and more determined effort. He loved the excitements of political controversy, and was perfectly at home on the hustings. Among the rude, reckless miners and squatters, in the diggings and ranches of the Golden State, he was always a popular stump speaker, though but few of them felt any sympathy for the political principles he so ably advocated. "Those who are acquainted only with his more grave senatorial efforts, can form no adequate idea of the ready, sparkling, ebulliant wit —the glancing and playful satire, mirthful while merciless—the keen syllogisms, and the sharp sophisms whose fallacies, though undiscoverable, were preplexing—and the sudden splendors of eloquence that formed the wonderful charm of his back-woods harangues. His fame became co-extensive with the coast; and the people in allusion to his gray bald head, which all knew, used to call him the 'Gray Eagle.'"*

HIS CELEBRATED ORATION ON THE DEATH OF SENATOR BRODERICK.

On the 16th of September, 1859, Senator David C. Broderick, the chief of the Douglas Democracy in California, fell mortally wounded in a duel with Judge Terry,

---

*Sketch of Col. Baker, by John Hay. Harpers' Magazine for December, 1861.

of the same State,—who was a prominent adherent of the Buchanan, or administration wing of that party. This unfortunate conflict was engendered by the use of unguarded expressions of a personal character, by the deceased, towards Judge Terry, which were inflamed by the bitter political contest then just terminated in that State. Colonel Baker had been associated with Broderick in the campaign, and was also one of his warmest personal friends. By common consent he now became the funeral orator.

The body of the stricken Senator was conveyed from the bloody field to the central Plaza of San Francisco, clad in the habiliments of the grave. The news of his tragic fate had spread rapidly through the streets and lanes of that crowded city, creating a profound sensation. A vast concourse of people soon thronged the square, and stood with awe-struck and solemn mien, in the presence of the lifeless form of the Tribune. Aloft the bells were ringing mournfully, "and their wild lament floating down to earth, deepened the emotion of the hour." The sad, unusual, and most impressive scene, was one well calculated to inspire the orator to the highest exertion of his powers. It bore no faint resemblance to another and greater spectacle, in another country, and more heroic age, when Mark Antony stood over the mangled corpse of the great Caesar, in the Roman Forum, and pronounced that matchless funeral oration, which has been so beautifully embalmed in verse by the immortal bard of Avon.

Amidst the silence, and subdued grief of the multitude, Colonel Baker rose and said:

"Citizens of California! A Senator lies dead in our midst. He is wrapped in a bloody shroud, and we to whom his toils and cares were given, are about to bear him to the place appointed for all the living. It is not fit that such a man should pass to the tomb unheralded; it is not fit that such a life should steal unnoticed to its close; it is not fit that such a death should call forth no rebuke, or be surrounded by no public lamentation. It is this conviction which impells the gathering of this assemblage. We are here of every station and pursuit, of every creed and character, each in his capacity of citizen, to swell the mournful tribute which the majesty of the people offers to the unreplying dead. He lies to-day surrounded by little funeral pomp. No banners droop above the bier; no melancholy music floats upon the reluctant air. The hopes of high-hearted friends droop like the fading flowers upon his breast, and the struggling sigh compels the tear in eyes that seldom weep. Around him are those who have known him best, and loved him longest; who have shared the triumph and endured the defeat. Near him are the gravest and noblest of the State, possessed by a grief at once earnest and sincere, while beyond, the masses of the people, whom he loved, and for whom his life was given, gather like a thunder-cloud of swelling and indignant grief. In such a presence, fellow citizens, let us linger for a moment at the portals of the tomb, whose shadowy arches vibrate to the public heart, to speak a few brief words of the man, of his life, and of his death.

"Mr. Broderick was born in the District of Columbia, in 1819; he he was of Irish descent, and of respectable, though obscure parentage; he had little of early advantages, and never summoned to his aid a complete and finished education. His boyhood—as indeed his early manhood—was passed in the city of New York, and the loss of his father early stimulated him to the efforts which maintained his surviving mother and brother, and served also to fix and form his character, even in his boyhood. His love for his mother was his first and most distinctive trait of character; and when his brother died—an early and sudden death—the shock gave a serious and reflective cast to his habits and his thoughts, which marked them to the last hours of his life.

"He was always filled with pride, and energy, and ambition; his pride was in the manliness and force of his character, and no man had more reason. His energy was manifest in the most resolute struggles with poverty and obscurity, and his ambition impelled him to seek a foremost place in the great race of honorable power. Up to the time of his arrival in California, his life had been passed amid events incident to such a character. Fearless, self-reliant, open in his enmities, warm in his friendship, wedded to his opinions, and marching directly to his purpose, through, and over all opposition, his career was chequered with success and defeat. But even in defeat his energies were strengthened and his character developed. When he reached these shores, his keen observation taught him at once, that he trod a broad field, and that a high career was before him. He had no false pride—sprang from a people, and of a race, whose vocation was labor— he toiled with his own hands, and sprang at a bound, from the workshop to the legislative hall. From that hour, there congregated around him, and against him, the elements of success and defeat—strong friendships, bitter enmities, high praise and malignant calumnies ; but he trod with a free and a proud step that onward path which has led him to glory and the grave.

"It would be idle for me, at this hour, and in this place, to speak of all that history with unmitigated praise ; it will be idle for his enemies hereafter to deny his claim to noble virtues and high purposes. When in the Legislature, he boldly denounced the special legislation, which is the curse of a new country, he proved his courage and his rectitude. When he opposed the various and sometimes successful schemes to strike out the salutary provisions of the constitution which guarded free labor, he was true to all the better instincts of his life. When prompted by his ambition and the admiration of his friends, he first sought a seat in the Senate of the United States, he sought the highest of all positions by legitimate effort, and failed with honor. It is my duty to say, that, in my judgment, when, at a later period he sought to anticipate the Senatorial election, he committed an error, which I think he lived to regret. It would have been a violation of the true principles of representative government, which no reason, public or private, could justify, and could never have met the permanent approval of good and wise men. Yet, while I say this over his bier, let me remind you of the temptation to such an error, of the plans and reasons which prompted it, and of the many good purposes it was intended to effect. And if ambition, the 'last infirmity of noble minds,' led him for a moment from the better path, let me remind you how nobly he returned to it. It is impossible to speak, within the limits of this address, of the events of that session of the Legislature at which he was elected to the Senate of the United States; but some things should not be passed in silence here. The contest between himself and the present Senator had been bitter and personal. He had triumphed; he had been powerfully sustained by his friends, and stood confessedly the 'first in honor, and the first in place.' He yielded to an appeal made to his magnanimity by his foe. If he judged unwisely, he has paid the forfeit well. Never in the history of political warfare, has any man been so pursued. Never has malignity so exhausted itself.

"Fellow citizens, the man who lies before you was your Senator. From the moment of his election, his character has been malinged, his motives attacked, his courage impeached, his patriotism assailed. It has been a system tending to one end, *and the end is here*. What was his crime? Review his history, consider his public acts, weigh his private character, and before the grave encloses him forever, judge between him and his enemies. As a man to be judged in his private relations, who was his superior? It was his boast—and amid the general license of a new country, it was a proud one—that his most scrutinizing enemy, could fix no single act of immorality upon him.

Temperate, decorous, self-restrained, he had passed through all the excitements of California unstained. No man could charge him with broken faith or violated trust. Of habits simple and inexpensive, he had no lust of gain. He overreached no man's weakness in a bargain, and withheld no man his just dues. Never, in the history of the State, has there been a citizen who has borne public relations more stainless in all respects than he. But it is not by this standard he is to be judged. He was a public man, and his memory demands a public judgment. What was his public crime? The answer is in his own words: 'They have killed me because I was opposed to the extention of slavery, and a corrupt administration.' Fellow citizens, they are remarkable words, uttered at a very remarkable moment; they involve the history of his Senatorial career, and of its sad and bloody termination. When Mr. Broderick entered the Senate, he had been elected at the beginning of a Presidential term as a friend of the President elect, having undoubtedly been one of his most influential supporters. There were, unquestionably, some things in the exercise of the appointing power which he could have wished otherwise ; but he had every reason with the Administration which could be supposed to weigh with a man in his position. He had heartily maintained the doctrine of popular sovereignty as set forth in the Cincinnati platform, and he never wavered in his support till the day of his death. But, when, in his judgement the President betrayed his obligations to the party and the country ; when, in the whole series of acts in relation to Kansas, he proved recreant to his pledges and instructions ; when the whole power of the Administration was brought to bear upon the legislative branch of the Government in order to force slavery upon an unwilling people, then, in the high performance of his duty as a Senator, he rebuked the Administration by his voice, and his vote, and stood by his principles. It is true he adopted no halfway measures. He threw the whole weight of his character into the ranks of the opposition ; he endeavored to rouse the people to an indignant sense of the iniquitous tyranny of the Federal power, and kindling with the contest, became its fiercest and firmest opponent.

" Fellow citizens, whatever may have been your political predilections, it is impossible to repress your admiration as you review the conduct of the man who lies hushed in death before you. You read in his history a glorious imitation of the great popular leader who opposed the despotic influence of power in other lands and in our own. When John Hampden died, at Chalgrovefield, he sealed his devotion to popular liberty with his blood. The eloquence of Fox found the source of its inspiration in his love of the people. When Senators conspired against Tiberius Gracchus, and the Tribune of the people fell beneath their daggers, it was power that prompted the crime and demanded the sacrifice. Who can doubt, if your Senator had surrendered his free thoughts, and bent in submission to the rule of the Administration, who can doubt that instead of resting on a bloody bier, he would this day have been reposing in the inglorious felicitude of Presidential sunshine ?

"Fellow citizens, let no man suppose that the death of the eminent citizen of whom I speak, was caused by any other reason than that to which his own words assign it. It has been long foreshadowed. It was predicted by his friends; it was threatened by his enemies; it was the consequence of intense political hatred. His death was a political necessity, poorly veiled under the guise of a private quarrel. Here, in his own State, among those who witnessed the late canvass, who knew the contending leaders—among those who knew the antagonists on the bloody ground, here the public conviction is so thoroughly settled, that nothing need be said. Tested by the correspondence itself, there was no cause in morals, in honor, in taste, by any code, by the custom of any civilized land, there was no cause for blood. Let me repeat the story; it is brief as it is fatal: a Judge of the Supreme Court descends into a political convention—it is just, however, to say that the occasion was to return thanks to his friends for an unsuccessful support. In a speech bitter and personal, he stigmatized Senator Broderick and all his friends in words of contemptuous insult. When Mr. Broderick saw that speech, he retorted, saying, in substance, that he had heretofore spoken of Judge Terry as an honest man, but that he now took it back. When inquired of, he admitted that he had so said, and connected his words with Judge Terry's speech as prompting them. So far as Judge Terry, personally, was concerned, this was the cause of mortal combat; there was no other. In the contest, which has just terminated in the State, Mr. Broderick had taken a leading part; he had been engaged in controversies very personal in their nature, because the subjects of public discussion had involved the character and conduct of many public and distinguished men. But Judge Terry was not one of them. He was no contestant; his conduct was not at issue; he had been mentioned but once incidentally—in reply to his own attack—and, except as it might be found in his peculiar traits, or peculiar fitness, there was no reason to suppose that he would seek any man's blood. When William of Nassau, the deliverer of Holland, died in the presence of his wife and children, the hand that struck the blow was not nerved by private vengeance. When the fourth Henry passed unharmed amid the dangers of the field of Ivry,

5

to perish in the streets of his capital by a fanatic, he did not seek to avenge a private grief. An exaggerated sense of personal honor—a weak mind with choleric passions, intense sectional prejudice, united with great confidence in the use of arms—these sometimes serve to stimulate the instruments which accomplish the deepest and deadliest purposes.

" Fellow citizens! One year ago I performed a duty such as I perform to-day, over the remains of Senator Ferguson,* who died as Broderick died, tangled in the meshes of the code of honor. To-day there is another and more eminent sacrifice. To-day I renew my protest; to-day I utter yours. The code of honor is a delusion and a snare; it palters with the hope of a true courage, and binds it at the feet of crafty and cruel skill. It surrounds its victim with the pomp and grace of the procession, but leaves him bleeding on the altar. It substitutes cold and deliberate preparations for courageous and manly impulse, and arms the one to disarm the other; it may prevent fraud between practiced duelists, who should be forever without its pale, but it makes the mere ' trick of the weapon' superior to the noblest cause and the truest courage. Its pretence of equality is a lie; it is equal in all the form, it is unjust in all the substance—the habitude of arms, the early training, the frontier life, the border war, the sectional custom, the life of leisure—all these are advantages which no negotiations can neutralize, and which no courage can overcome.

" But, fellow citizens, the protest is not only spoken in your words and mine; it is written in indelible characters; it is written in the blood of Gilbert, in the blood of Furguson, in the blood of Broderick, and the inscription will not altogether fade. With the administration of the code in this particular case, I am not here to deal. Amid passionate grief let us strive to be just. I give no currency to the rumors of which personally I know nothing; there are other tribunals to which they may well be referred, and this is not one of them; but I am here to say that whatever in the code of honor or out of it demands or allows a deadly combat, where there is not in all things entire and

---

*Formerly a brilliant young lawyer of Springfield, Illinois.

certain equality, is a prostitution of the name, is an invasion of the substance, and is a shield blazoned with the name of chivalry to cover the malignity of murder. And now, as the shadows turn towards the East, and we prepare to bear these poor remains to their silent resting place, let us not seek to repress the generous pride which prompts a recital of noble deeds and manly virtues. He rose unaided and alone; he began his career without family or fortune, in the face of difficulties; he inherited poverty and obscurity; he died a Senator in Congress, having written his name in the history of the great struggle for the rights of the people against the despotism of organization, and the corruption of power. He leaves in the hearts of his friends the tenderest and the proudest of recollections. He was honest, faithful, earnest, sincere, generous and brave; he felt in all the great crises of his life that he was a leader in the ranks, and for the rights of the masses of men, and he could not falter.

"When he returned from that fatal field, while the dark wing of the archangel of death was casting her shadows upon his brow, his greatest anxiety was as to the performance of his duty. He felt that all his strength, and all his life, belonged to the cause to which he had devoted them.

"'Baker,' said he—and to me they were his last words—'Baker, when I was struck, I tried to stand firm, but the blow blinded me, and I could not.' I trust that it is no shame to my manhood to say, that tears blinded me as he said it.

"Of his last hours, I have no heart to speak. He was the last of his race; there was no kindred hand to smooth his couch, or wipe the death-damps from his brow; but around that dying bed, strong men, the friends of early manhood, the devoted adherents of later life, bowed in irrepressible grief, and lifted up their voices and wept.

"But, fellow citizens, the voice of lamentation is not uttered by private friendship alone; the blow that struck his manly breast, has touched the heart of a people, and as the sad tidings spread, a general gloom prevails. Who now shall speak for California? Who be the interpreter of the wants of the Pacific coast? Who can appeal to the

communities of the Atlantic who love free labor? Who can speak for
the masses of men, with a passionate love for the classes from whence
he sprung? Who can defy the blandishments of power, the indolence
of office, the corruption of administrations? What hopes are buried
with him in the grave?

> "Ah! who that gallant spirit shall resume,
> Leap from Eurota's bank and call us from the tomb."

*" But the last word must be spoken, and the imperious mandate of death
must be fulfilled. Thus, O! brave heart, we bear thee to thy rest! Thus,
surrounded by tens of thousands, we leave thee to the equal grave. As in
life no other voice among us so rang its trumpet blast upon the ear of freemen, so in death its echoes will reverberate amid our mountains and valleys,
until truth and valor cease to appeal to the human heart.*

> His love of truth, too warm, too strong,
> For hope or fear to chain or chill,
> His hate of tyranny and wrong,
> Burn in the breast he kindled still.
> *" Good friend! true hero! hail and farewell."*

This brilliant and thrilling eulogy has been more
universally read and admired than any other effort of
Baker's oratorical genius. His more enthusiastic friends
have not hesitated to pronounce it a master-piece of its
kind, rivalling in its exquisitly moulded sentences and
classical finish, the productions of the most celebrated
orators of antiquity. More discerning critics, however, deem this rather extravagant laudation, and assail
the speech on account of its strong partisan spirit.
And yet, in almost all the essentials of a great oration
—in its method and arrangement, in force of thought,
in elevation of style, in appositeness of historical illustration, and above all, in the depth and energy of feeling

displayed—it would be difficult to find its superior among the records of modern oratory. Baker seemed to have loved Broderick as a brother—indeed, there was much in common between them—and hence mourned his untimely fall, with an eloquence and a pathos, which none but himself could command. We cannot too highly commend his indignant protest— the expression of a matured opinion—against duelling, or the so-called "code of honor," which has been justly termed the "inhuman relic of a barbarous age."

HE GOES TO OREGON—IS ELECTED TO THE UNITED STATES SENATE.

Failing to realize his hopes of high political advancement in California, Colonel Baker, shortly after the unhappy death of Broderick, changed his residence to the younger and more remote commonwealth of Oregon. He immediately entered with might and main upon the political canvass then in progress in that State. There were three tickets in the field—the Administration, the Douglas, and the Republican. After a hard struggle, the opposition to the Administration carried the Legislature; but a coalition had to be formed among them in order to elect a United States Senator. And now came the great crisis of Baker's political life. David Logan, Esq., a son of Judge Logan of Illinois, was generally believed to be the first choice of the Republican members. He was a gentleman of distinguished ability as a lawyer; had lived in the Territory several years before it became a State; was thoroughly acquainted with the wants of its people, and had endeared himself to them by his vigorous, though unsuccessful races for Congress. The Administration Democrats, who constituted a formidable minority in the Legislative body, also made a sturdy fight, and when the question came to a vote, some of them "took to the bush."

But the commanding reputation of Colonel Baker, combined with his experience and dexterity as a political manager, and the singular fascination of his address, finally overcame all opposition, and he bore off the glittering Senatorial prize.

He had now reached the eminence for which he had struggled through many long years, against the adverse winds and waves of fortune. He had now attained the highest civic honor to which his nativity would permit him to aspire—and still he was not content.

Returning to San Francisco, on his way to the East, Col. Baker was the recipient of a public ovation, on which occasion he made a speech of wondrous eloquence. It was known that he had been elected to the Senate by a coalition, and it was surmised by some of his political friends that he might, in consequence, prove recreant to, or at least lukewarm in the advocacy of the great principles of freedom, free labor, &c. To disabuse the public mind of any such impression, he now, in terms of fiery and impassioned rhetoric, renewed his fealty to those principles which he claimed had given direction to his whole political life. The subjoined brief passage exemplifies his position:

"As for me, I dare not, will not, be false to freedom. Where the feet of my youth were planted, there by freedom my feet shall ever stand. I will walk beneath her banner. I will glory in her strength. I have seen her in history struck down on a hundred fields of battle. I have seen her friends fly from her, her foes gather around her. I have seen her bound to a stake. I have seen them give her ashes to the winds. But when they turned to exult, I have seen her again meet them face to face, resplendent in complete steel, brandishing in her strong right hand a flaming sword, red with insufferable light. I take courage. The people gather around her. The genius of America will yet lead her sons to freedom."

In December, 1860, while en-route to Washington, Colonel Baker paid a hasty visit to Springfield, Illinois, his old home, where he was honored with a public reception. On behalf of the citizens, the Hon. J. C. Conkling, in a neat and tasteful speech, formally welcomed him to the scene of his early labors and triumphs. The Senator elect responded in characteristic style. He expressed the liveliest gratitude at the heartiness and enthusiasm with which he had been received by his old friends, without distinction of party; referred in touching language to his previous history; alluded to the wonderful growth and prosperity of Illinois, and of the great West; and spoke with solicitude of our national difficulties, and the then impending civil war.

He was now verging close on fifty; and about his bodily presence there was that air of blended grace and dignity, which betokened something more than an ordinary man. Of medium height, his figure was still erect, and roundly and compactly built. His head (which might have formed a model for a sculptor) was partially bald, and his hair and small side whiskers almost white. His complexion was florid; his nose, large and long, was of the Roman type; his eyes of a grayish tint, and capable of expressing every varying emotion of the soul. His manners were easy and urbane, whilst his voice was penetrating and finely modulated, as in the days of yore.

On taking his seat in the Senate, Mr. Baker entered industriously upon the discharge of the responsible duties of his station, and ranked from the outset among the foremost orators and debaters in that dignified assembly. "For the first time in his life," says the sketch from which we have already quoted, "he was placed in a position which was entirely appropriate to him. The decorum and courtesy that usually marks the intercourse of Senators, was most grateful to his habits of thought and feeling. The higher range of discussion, and the more cultivated tone of sentiment and discourse prevalent there, gave him an opportunity that all his life had lacked, of doing his best among his equals. Among these refined members, of the most august of representative assemblies, there was none more courteous, more polished, than this Western lawyer, this rouser of the dwellers in the backwoods."

His remarkably fluent, graceful and natural style of oratory, showed that he had closely followed, if he had not attentively studied, Hamlet's advice to the players. Listen, for a moment, to the great teacher, whose words of wisdom are alike applicable to orators and actors:

"Speak the piece, I pray you, as I pronounce it to you, trippingly on the tongue; but if you mouth it as many of our players do, I had as lief the town crier spoke my lines. Nor do not saw the air too much with your hands, thus; but use all gently; for in the very torrent, tempest, and (as I may say) whirlwind of your passion, you must acquire and beget a temperance that may give it smoothness. O! it offends me to the soul to hear a robustious periwig-pated fellow tear a passion to tatters, to very rags, to split the ears of groundlings; who, for the most part, are incapable of nothing but inexplicable dumb shows and noise. I would have such a fellow whipped for overdoing Termagant; it out Herods Herod. Pray you avoid it. Be not too tame neither, but let your own discretion be your tutor; suit the action to the word, the word to the action; with this special observation, that you overstep not the modesty of nature; for anything so overdone is from the purpose of playing, whose end both at the first, and now, was, and is, to hold as 'twere the mirror up to nature, to show virtue her own feature, scorn her own image, and the very age and body of the time his form and pressure."

HIS GREAT SPEECH IN THE SENATE.

On the 2d and 3d days of January, 1861, Senator Baker addressed the Senate at great length upon a joint resolution which had been offered by Senator, (afterwards President) Johnson, of Tennessee, proposing certain amendments to the Federal Constitution. The importance of the subject, and the fame of the orator, attracted a dense crowd to the Capitol. The galleries and corridors of the Senate Chamber were thronged with eager listeners during the whole time occupied in the delivery of his speech. The Senator spoke in reply to an elaborate effort of the Hon. J. P. Benjamin, of Louisiana, and he adopted much the same line of argument as that pursued by Webster, in his famous reply to Hayne, in 1832. For want of adequate space, we can only reproduce some of the more important portions of this exhaustive speech, including his magnificent exordium and peroration:

"Mr. President: The adventurous traveller, who wanders on the slopes of the Pacific and on the very verge of civilization, stands awestruck and astonished in that great chasm formed by the torrent of the Columbia, as, rushing between Mt. Hood and Mt. St. Helena, it breaks through the ridges of the Cascade Mountains to find the sea. Nor is this wonder lessened when he hears his slightest tones repeated and re-echoed with a larger utterance in the reverberations which lose themselves at last amid the surrounding and distant hills. So I, standing on this spot, and speaking for the first time in this Chamber, reflect with astonishment that my feeblest word is re-echoed, even while I speak, to the confines of the Republic. I trust, sir, that in so speaking in the midst of such an auditory, and in the presence of great events, I may remember all the responsibility these impose upon me, to perform my duty to the Constitution of the United States, and to be in nowise forgetful of my obligations to the whole country, of which I am a devoted and affectionate son.

"It is my purpose to reply as best I may, to the speech of the honorable and distinguished Senator from the State of Louisiana. I do so, because in my judgment at least, it is the ablest speech I have heard, perhaps the ablest speech I will hear upon that side of the question; and in that view of the subject, because it is respectful in tone, and elevated in sentiment and manner; and because, while it will be my fortune to differ from him on many, nay, on most of the points to which he has addressed himself, yet it is not, I trust, inappropriate for me to say, that much of what he has said, and the manner in which he has said it, has tended to increase the personal respect, nay, the admiration, which I have learned to feel for him. But, sir, while I say this, I am reminded of the saying of a great man, (Dr. Johnson) who, when he was asked his critical opinion of a book just then published, and which was making a great sensation in London, said, 'Sir, the fellow who wrote that work, has done very well what nobody ought ever to do at all.'

"The entire object of this speech is, as I understand it, to offer a philosophical and constitutional disquisition to prove that the government of these United States, is, in point of fact, no government at all; that it has no principle of vitality; that it is to be overthrown by a touch; dwindled into insignificance, dissolved by a breath; not by maladministration merely, but in consequence of organic defects interwoven with its very existence. But sir, this purpose, strange and mournful in anybody,—still more so in him—this purpose has a terrible significance now and here. In the judgment of the honorable Senator, the Union is this day dissolved; it is broken and disintegrated; civil war is at once a consequence necessary and inevitable. Standing in the Senate Chamber, he speaks like a prophet of woe. The burden of his prediction is the echo of what the distinguished Senator, now in that chair, (Mr. Iverson) has said before: "too late, too late." The gleaming and lurid lights of war flash around his brow, even while he speaks; and, sir, if it were not for the exquisite amenity of his tone and manner, we could easily persuade ourselves that we saw the flashing of the armor of the soldier, beneath the robe of the senator.

"My purpose is far distant, sir; I think it is far higher. I desire to contribute my poor argument to maintain the dignity, the honor of the Government under which I live, and under whose august shadow I hope to die. I propose, in opposition to all that has been said, to show that the government of the United States is in very deed and fact, a real, and substantial power; ordained by the people, not dependent on the States; sovereign in its sphere—a union, and not a compact between sovereign States; that, according to its true theory, it has the inherent power of self-preservation; that its constitution is a perpetuity, beneficent, unfailing, grand; and that its powers are equally capable of exercise against domestic treason, and against a foreign foe. Such, sir, is the main purpose of my speech; and what I may say in addition to this, will be drawn from me in reply to the speech to which I propose now to address myself.

" Sir, the argument of the honorable Senator from Louisiana, is addressed first, to establish the proposition that the State of South Carolina has, as she says, seceded from the Union rightfully; and sir, just here he says one thing which meets my hearty approval and acquiescence. He says he does not deem it—such is the substance of his remark—unwise or improper to argue the right of the case, even now, and here. In this I agree with him most heartily. Right and duty are always majestic ideas. They march, an invisible guard, in the van of all true progress; they animate the loftiest spirit in the public assemblies; they nerve the arm of the warrior; they kindle the soul of the statesman, and the imagination of the poet; they sweeten every reward, they console every defeat. Sir, they are of themselves an indissoluble chain which binds feeble, erring humanity to the eternal throne of God.

" I observe first, sir, that the argument of the gentleman, from beginning to end, is based upon the assumption that the Constitution of the United States is a compact between sovereign States. I think I in no sense misapprehend it; I am sure such cannot be my desire. I understood him throughout the whole tone of his speech to maintain that proposition—I repeat it, that the Constitution of the United States is a compact between sovereign States. Arguing from thence he arrives at the conclusion, that being so, a compact when broken by either of the States, or by the General Government, the creature of the Constitution, South Carolina may treat the compact as so broken, the contract as rescinded; may withdraw peacefully from the Union, and resume her original condition.

" I remark next, that this proposition is in nowise new; and perhaps for that, as it is a constitutional proposition, it is all the better. Again, the argument by which the honorable Senator seeks to maintain it is in nowise new in any of its parts. I have examined with some care the arguments hitherto made by great men, the echoes of whose eloquence still linger under this dome, and I find that the proposition, the argument, the authority, the illustration, are but a repetition of the famous discussion led off by Mr. Calhoun, and growing out of the attempt of South Carolina to do before, what she says she has done now. ' If the proposition is not new, and if the arguments are not strange, it will not be wonderful if the replies partake of the like character. I deny, as Mr. Madison denied, I deny, as Mr. Webster denied, I deny, as General Jackson denied, that this Union is a compact between the sovereign States at all ; and so denying, I meet just [here the authorities which the honorable Senator has chosen to quote. They are substantially as follows : first, not the Constitution itself, (and that is remarkable,) second, not the arguments made by the great expounders of the Constitution directly upon this floor ; but mainly fugitive expressions, sometimes hasty, not always considered, on propositions not germane to the controversy now engaging us to-day ; and when made, if misapprehended, corrected again and again in after years. To illustrate : The gentleman from Louisiana has quoted at considerable length from the debates in the Convention which formed the Federal Constitution ; he has quoted the opinions of Mr. Madison, and to those who have not looked into the question, it might appear as if those expressions were really in support of the proposition, that this is a compact between sovereign States. Now sir, to show that that is in no sense so, I will read as a reply to the entire quotations of Mr. Madison, what Mr. Madison has said upon that subject, upon the fullest consideration. I proceed to read the letter of Mr. Madison to Mr. Webster, dated March 15th, 1833."

Having read the letter referred to, Mr. Baker continued : " I submit to the candor of the Senator from Louisiana, that this is distinct, positive, unequivocal authority to show that so far as the opinions of Mr. Madison were concerned, he did not believe that the Constitution

of the United States was a compact between sovereign States ; but
that he did believe it was a form of Government ordained by the
people of the United States.

" Again, Mr. Webster is quoted. I expected when I heard Mr.
Webster named, that the honorable Senator would allude to the great
discussion which his genius has rendered immortal. He does not do
that, but refers specifically to a passage of Mr. Webster in an argument, I believe, upon a question arising as to the boundary between
Massachusetts and Rhode Island."

The speaker quoted in succession the opinions of Mr. Webster, Mr.
Adams, and General Jackson, in support of his proposition, comment-
ing on the same, and then proceeded with his argument on this branch
of the subject as follows : " Another mistake which I think is obvious
throughout the speech of the Senator from Louisiana, is the assumption,
not only that the Constitution is a compact, but that the States as
parties to it are sovereign. Sir, they are not sovereign ; and this
Federal Government is not sovereign. Paraphrasing the Mahometan
expression, "There is but one God," I may and do say, not without
reverence, there is but one sovereign, and that sovereign is the people.
The State Government is its creation ; the Federal Government is its
creation ; each supreme in its sphere ; each sovereign for its purpose ;
but each limited in its authority, and each dependent on delegated
power. Why sir, can that State—either Oregon or South Carolina—
be sovereign which relinquishes the insignia of sovereignty, the exercise of its highest powers, the expression of its noblest dignities ? Not
so. We can neither coin money, nor buy impost duties, nor make
war, nor peace, nor raise standing armies, nor build fleets, nor issue
bills of credit. In short, sir, we cannot do—because the people, as
sovereigns, have placed the power in other hands—many, nay, most of
those things which exhibit and proclaim the sovereignty of a State to
the whole world. Mr. Webster has well observed that there can be in
this country no sovereignty in the European sense of sovereignty. It
is, I believe, a feudal idea. It has no place here. I repeat, we are
not sovereign here. They are not sovereign in South Carolina, and

cannot be in the nature of the case ; and therefore all assumptions and all presumptions arising out of the proposition of sovereignty on the part or a State is a fallacy from beginning to end.

" Again sir, Mr. Calhoun, in the course of his celebrated argument, in well chosen words, insisted that the States in their sovereign capacity, acceded to a compact. Mr. Webster replied with his usual force. The word " accede" was chosen as the converse of " secede ;" the argument being intended to be that, if the State accedes to a compact, she may secede from that compact. But said Mr. Webster —and no man has answered the argument, and no man ever will—it is not the accession to a compact at all ; it is not the formation of a league at all ; it is the action of the people of the United States, carrying into effect their purpose from the Declaration of Independence itself, manifested in the ordination and establishment of a Government, and expressed in their own emphatic words in the preamble of the Constitution of the United States.

" In arguing upon the meaning and import of the Constitution, I had hoped that a lawyer so distinguished as the gentleman from Louisiana, would have referred to the terms of that document, to have endeavored at least, to find its real meaning from its force and mode of expression. In the absence of such quotation, I beg leave to remind him that the Constitution itself declares by whom it was made, and for what it was made. Mr. Adams, reading it, declares that the Constitution of the United States was the work of one people—the people of the United States—and that these United States still continue one people ; and to establish that, among other things, he refers to the fact—the great, the patent, the glorious fact—that the Constitution declares itself to have been made by the people, and not by sovereign States—by the people of the United States; not a compact, not a league, but it declares that the people of the United States do ordain and establish a Government. Now I ask the Senator what becomes of the reiteration that the Constitution is a compact between sovereign States.

" Pursuing what I think is a defective mode of reasoning from beginning to end, the distinguished Senator from Louisiana quotes

Vattel, and for what? To prove what, as I understand, nobody denies, that a sovereign State being sovereign, may make a compact, and afterwards withdraw from it. Our answer to that is that South Carolina is not a sovereign State; that South Carolina has not made a compact, and that therefore she cannot withdraw from it; and I submit that all the disquisitions upon the nature of European sovereignty, or any of those forms of government to which the distinguished Senator has had his observation attracted, are no argument whatever in a controversy as to the force and meaning of our Constitution, bearing upon the States, sovereign in some sense, not sovereign in others, but bearing most upon individuals in their individual relations. But the object of the speech was two-fold. It was to prove first that the Union was a compact between States, and that, therefore, there was a rightful remedy for injury, intolerable or otherwise, by secession. Now, sir, I confess, in one thing I do not understand this speech, although it is so clearly uttered and forcibly expressed. Does the Senator mean to argue that there is such a thing as a Constitutional right of secession. Is it a right under the Constitution, or is it a right above it and beyond it?"

In a running debate with Senator Benjamin, Mr. Baker next discussed the Constitutional right of secession, showing its fallacy, and then, passing to the question of the revolutionary right of a people to change their form of government, he said:

"I admit that there is a revolutionary right. Whence does it spring? How is it limited? To these questions, for a moment I address myself. Whence does it spring? Why, sir, as a right in communities, it is of the same nature as the right of self-preservation in the individual. A community protects itself by revolution against intolerable oppression, against any form of government, as an individual protects himself against intolerable oppression by brute force. No compact, no treaty, no constitution, no form of government, no oath or obligation can deprive a man or a community of that sacred ultimate right. Now, sir, I think I state that proposition as fully as I could be desired to state it by the gentlemen on the other side. The question that arises between us at once, is, how this right of revolution must be exercised? In a case, and in a case only, where all other remedies fail; where the oppression is grinding, intolerable, and permanent; where revolution is in its nature a fit redress; and where they who adopt it as a remedy, can do it in the full light of all the examples of the past; of all the responsibilities of the present; of all the unimpassioned judgment of the future, and the ultimate determination of the Supreme Arbitrator and Judge of all. Sir, a right so exercised, is a sacred right. I maintain it; and I would exercise it. The question recurs: has South Carolina that right? I think the honorable Senator will not deny that one of the greatest responsibilities which could devolve upon a community or State, is to break up an established peaceful form of government. If that be true as an abstract proposition, how much more does the truth strike us, when we apply it to the condition in which we found ourselves two months ago? South Carolina proposes now, according to the latter doctrine, to secede as a revolutionary right, as a resistance against intolerable oppression; as an appeal to arms for the maintenance of rights, for the redress of wrongs, where the one cannot be maintained, and the other redressed otherwise. Now, sir, I demand of her, and of those who defend her, that she should stand out in the broad light of history, and declare, if not by the Senators that she ought to have on this floor, by those who league with her, in what that oppression consists; where that injury is inflicted; by whom the blow is struck; what weapon is used in the attack. So much, at least, we have the right to inquire. After that inquiry, permit me to add another thing: a State claiming to be sovereign, and a people, part of a great Government, ought to act with deliberation and dignity; she ought to be able to appeal to all history for kindred cases of intolerable oppression, and kindred occasions of magnanimous revolution.

" Sir, we are not unacquainted in this Chamber with the history of revolutions. We very well know that our forefathers rebelled against the house of Stuart. And why? The causes are as well known to the world, as the great struggle by which they maintained the right, and the great renown which has ever followed the deed. When Oliver Cromwell brought a traitorous, false king, and gave him, a dim discrowned monarch, to the block, he did it by a solemn judgment, in the face of man, and in the face of Heaven, avouching the deed on the great doctrine of revolutionary right; and although a fickle people betrayed his memory—although the traditions of monarchy were yet too strong for the better thought of the English people—yet still, now, here, to-day, wherever the English language is read, wherever that historic glowing story is repeated, the hearts of brave and generous men throb when the deed is avouched, and justify the act. Again, there was a second revolution, the revolution of 1688, and why? Because a cowardly, fanatic, bigoted monarch, sought by the exercise of a power, to be used through the bayonets of standing armies, to repress the liberties of a free people; because he attempted to force upon them a religion alien to their thought and to their hope; because he attempted to trample under foot all that was sacred in the constitution of English government.

"And, sir, in the history of revolutions, there are examples more illustrious still; perhaps the greatest of them all, that revolution which ended in the establishment of the Dutch Republic. My honorable friend, I know, has read the glowing pages of Motley, perhaps the most accurate, if not the most brilliant, of American historians. I am sure that his heart has throbbed with generous enthusiasm, as he read the thrilling pages of that story, where a great people, led by the heroic house of Orange, pursued through danger, through sacrifice, through blood, through destruction of property, of houses, of families, and of all but the great indestructible spirit of liberty, the tenor of their way to liberty, and greatness and glory at last. Sir, I need not tell him the oppression against which they rebelled; that the intolerable tyranny under which they groaned, was of itself sufficient not only to enlist on their side, and in their behalf, all the sympathies of civilized Europe, but the sympathies of the whole civilized world, as they have read the story since.

"Yet, once more, in the full light of these revolutions, our forefathers rebelled against a tyrant, declaring the causes of the revolution, proclaiming them to the world, in a document that is familiar to us all. We recognize the right. Why? Because the oppression was intolerable, because the tyranny could not be borne; because the essential rights belonging to every human being were violated, and that continually, and in words more eloquent than I could use, or than I now have time to quote, Mr. Jefferson proclaimed them to the world, and gave the reasons which impelled us to the separation. Sir, I ask the honorable Senator to bring his record of reasons for revolution, bloodshed and war, here to-day, and compare them with that document."

He next reviewed in detail, the many grievancies of the South, Speaking of the right of free discussion, and of a free press, he eloquently said:

"Mr. President, do gentlemen propose to us seriously, that we shall stop the right of free discussion, that we shall limit the free press, that we shall restrain the expression of free opinion, everywhere, on all subjects, and at all times? Why, sir, in our land, if there be any base enough to blaspheme the Maker that created him, the Savior that died for him, we have no power to stop him. If there be the most bitter, unjust, and vehement denunciation of all principles of morality and goodness, on which human society is based, and on which it may securely stand, we have, for great and overruling reasons connected with liberty itself, no power to restrain it. Private character, public service, individual relations—neither of these, nor age, nor sex, can be, in the nature of our Government, exempt from that liability to attack. And, sir, shall gentleman complain that slavery shall not be made, and is not made an exception to that general rule? You did that when you made what you call a compact with us. You were then emerging out of the war of Independence. Your fathers had fought for that right, and more than that, they had declared that the violation of that right was one of the great causes which impelled them to the separation.

I submit these thoughts to gentlemen on the other side, in the candid hope that they will see at once, that the attempt to require us to do for them what we cannot do for ourselves, is unjust in the highest degree. Sir, the liberty of the press is the highest safeguard to all free government. Ours could not exist without it. It is with us, nay, with all men, like a great, exulting and abounding river. It is fed by the dews of heaven, which distil their sweetest drops to form it. It gushes from the rill, as it breaks from the deep caverns of the earth. It is fed by a thousand affluents that dash from the mountain top, to separate again into a thousand bounteous and irrigating rills around. On its broad bosom it bears a thousand barks. There Genius spreads its purpling sail; there Poetry dips its silver oar; there Art, Invention, Discovery, Science, Morality, Religion, may safely and securely float. It wanders through every land. It is a genial, cordial source of thought and inspiration, wherever it touches, whatever it surrounds. Sir, upon its borders grow every flower of grace, and every fruit of truth. I am not here to deny that that river sometimes oversteps its bounds. I am not here to deny that that stream sometimes becomes a dangerous torrent, and destroys towns and cities on its banks; but I am here to say, that without it, civilization, humanity, government, all that makes society itself, would disappear, and the world would return to its ancient barbarism. Sir, if that were to be possible, the fine conception of the great poet would be realized. If that were to be possible, though for a moment, *civilization itself would roll the wheels of its car backward for two thousand years.* Sir, if that were so, it would be true that

> "As one by one in dread Medea's train,
> Star after star fades off the etherial plain;
> Thus at her felt approach and secret might,
> Art after art goes out and all is night.
> Philosophy, that leaned on Heaven before,
> Sinks to her second cause and is no more;
> Religion, blushing, veils her sacred fires,
> And, unawares, morality expires."

" Sir, we will not risk these consequences, even for slavery; we will not risk these consequences even for Union; we will not risk these consequences to avoid that civil war with which you threaten us; that war which you announce as deadly, and which you declare to be inevitable."

Arguing the question of concession and compromise, he continued:

"Sir, while it is quite well that I should announce my opinion, as to what we might do, I shall enter into no details. I shall endeavor to bind nobody else. I express my conviction at the moment, subject of course to all the changes that events and circumstances hereafter to transpire, may justify. I will never yield to the idea that the great Government of this country shall protect slavery in any Territory now ours, or hereafter to be acquired. It is in my opinion a great principle of free government, not to be surrendered. It is the object of the great battle which we have fought, and which we have won. It is, in my poor opinion, the point upon which there is concord and agreement between the great masses of the North, who may agree in no other political opinion whatever. In my opinion, nine tenths of the entire population of the North and West, are devoted in the depth of their hearts to the great constitutional idea, that freedom is the rule, and that slavery is the exception; that it ought not to be extended by virtue of the powers of the Government of the United States, and come weal, come woe, it never shall be.

"But, sir, I add one other thing; when you talk to me about compromise or concession, I am not sure I always understand you. Do you mean that I am to give up my conviction of right? Armies cannot compel that in the breast of a free people. Do you mean that I am to concede the benefits of the political struggle through which we have passed, considered politically only? Do you mean that we are to deny the great principle upon which our political action has been based? You know we cannot. But if you mean by compromise and concession, to ask us to see whether or not we have been hasty, angry, passionate, excited, and in many respects violated your feelings, your character, your right of property, we will look; and as I said yesterday, if we have, *we will undo it.* Allow me to say again, if there be any lawyer, or any court, that will advise us that our laws are unconstitutional, we will repeal them. Such is my opinion.

"Now, as to territory, I will not yield one inch to secession; but there are things that I will yield. It is somewhere told, that when Harold of England received a messenger from a brother, with whom he was at variance, to inquire on what terms reconciliation and peace could be effected between brothers, he replied in a gallant and generous spirit, in a few words: 'The terms I offer, are, the affection of a brother, and the earldom of Northumberland.' * * Sir, in that spirit I speak. * * * * "I say that I will yield no inch, no word to the threat of secession, unconstitutional, revolutionary, unwise, at variance with the heart and the hope of all mankind but themselves. To that I yield nothing; but if the States loyal to the Constitution, if people magnanimous and just, desiring a return of paternal feeling, shall come to us and ask for peace, permanent, enduring peace and affection, and say, 'what will you grant?' I say to them, ask all that a gentleman ought to propose, and I will yield all that a gentleman ought to offer. Nay, more; if you are galled because we claim the right to prohibit slavery in territory now free, or in any Territory which acknowledges our jurisdiction, we will evade—I speak for myself—I will aid in evading that question. I will agree to make it all States, and let the people decide at once. I will agree to place them in that condition, where the prohibition will never be necessary to justify ourselves to our consciences, or to our constituents. I will agree to anything which is not to force upon me the necessity of protecting slavery in the name of freedom. To that I never can, and never will yield.

*　*　*　*　*　*　*　*　*　*　*　*

"Amid all the threats of dissolution, and all the croakings and predictions of evil, when the gentleman gets up inflamed by the momentary inspiration, and declares that there will be civil war, in the next, as he concludes in an expression full of pathos, he says: 'Let us depart in peace,' 'crying peace, when there is no peace.' Amid all this, I have great faith yet in the loyalty of the people of the South to the Union. I see around me to-day, that the clouds are breaking away. I see men of every shade of opinion on other subjects, agreeing in this one thing: that in secession there is danger and death. I see from 'Old Chippewa,' from Gen. Wool, from men of their high character, of their great age, of their proud career, of their enlarged patriotism, down to the

lower ranks of men who love the country and venerate the Constitution—
I see, and I hear everywhere, expressions that even yet fill the patriot
heart with hope, and I am not without hope that, when there is delay,
when time is allowed to the feverish sentiment to subside, and for
returning reason to resume its place, trusted to the people of this
whole Union, the Constitution will remain safe, unshaken forever ; yes,
sir, until

> " Wrapt in flames the realms of ether glow,
> And Heaven's last thunder shakes the world below."

On the much mooted question of " coercion," he thus
expressed his views, in a general way:

" Sir, as I approach a close, I am reminded that the honorable
Senator from Louisiana, has said in a tone which I by no means admire:
' Now gentlemen of the North, a State has seceded ; you must either
acknowledge her independence, or you must make war.' To that we
reply, we will take no counsel of our opponents. We will not acknowledge her independence. They say we cannot make war against the
State ; and the gentleman undertakes to ridicule the distinction which
we make between a State and individuals. Sir, it was a distinction
that Mr. Madison well understood ; it was a distinction that General
Jackson was very well determined to recognize ; it was the distinction
which was made in the whole argument when the Constitution was
formed, and I may say here, that all the arguments adduced by the
gentleman from Elliot's Debates, on the formation of the Constitution,
were arguments addressed against the propriety and wisdom of giving,
under the old patched up Confederation, power to the Government to
compel States, because they could not. They did not dare to do it,
for they did not choose to confound the innocent with the guilty, and
make war on some portion of unoffending people, because others were
guilty ; and therefore, among other reasons, the new Government was
formed, a Union—' a more perfect Union'—by one people. That is the
answer to the whole argument.

" Now, sir, let us examine for a moment, this idea that we cannot make war. First, we do not propose to do it. Does any gentleman on this side of the Chamber propose to declare war against South Carolina. Did you ever hear us suggest such a thing? You talk to us about coercion; many of you talk to us as if you desired us to attempt it. It would not be very strange if a Government, and hitherto a great Government, were to coerce obedience to her law, upon the part of them who were subject to her jurisdiction. No great cause of complaint in that, certainly. 'But,' says the gentleman, 'these persons offending against your law, are a sovereign State; you cannot make war upon her,' and following out with the acuteness of a lawyer, what he supposes to be the *modus operandi*, he asks, 'What will you do if you will not acknowledge her independence, and you do not make war; how will you collect the revenue?' And he goes on to show very conclusivsly, to his own mind, that we cannot. He shows us how a skillful lawyer, step by step, will interpose exception, motion, demurrer, rejoinder and sur-rejoinder, from the beginning to the end of the legal chapter; and says, with an air of triumph, which I thought did not become a gentleman that is still a Senator from a sovereign State, upon this floor, he says, 'it is nonsense; you cannot do it; you will not acknowledge her; you will not declare war; you cannot collect your revenue.' Sir, if that is the case to-day, it has been so for seventy years; we have been at the mercy of anybody and everybody who might choose to flout us. Is that true? Are we a Government? Have we the power to execute the laws? The gentleman threatens us with the consequences, and he says if we attempt it, there will be all sorts of legal delays interposed, and when that is done, there will be a mob; a great Government will be kicked out of existence by the tumultuous and vulgar feet of a mob, and he seems to rejoice at it. * * * * Why, Mr. President, against the legal objections to collecting the revenue in a case where South Carolina revolts, and individuals refuse to pay duties, against the lawyership of my friend from Louisiana, I will put another lawyer, General Jackson, a man of whom Mr. Webster said, that when he put his foot out, he never took it back; and if the gentleman wants a solution of the difficulties as to the manner in which the revenue is to be collected near the sovereign State of South Carolina, when she is in a condition of revolt or revolution, I will show him what General Jackson thought, and ordered to be done, when South Carolina revolted once before. I will read the instructions of General Jackson as to the mode of collecting the revenue, when South Carolina was preparing, by ordinance of nullification, to refuse to pay it.

* * * * * * * * * * * *

"Why, sir, there is nothing practical in this attempted idea that we cannot punish an individual, or that we cannot compel him to obey the law, because a sovereign State will succor him."

The orator concluded this luminous and comprehensive speech in the following lofty and impressive strain, adopting as his own, Webster's words of solemn import and burning eloquence:

"Whatever moderation, whatever that great healer, time, whatever the meditation of those allied to these people in blood, in sympathy, in interest, may effect, let that be done; but at last, let the laws be maintained, and the Union be preserved. At whatever cost, by whatever constitutional process, through whatever of darkness or danger there may be, let us proceed in the broad luminous path of duty, ' till danger's troubl'd night be passed, and the star of peace returns.'

"As I take my leave of a subject, upon which I have already detained you too long, I think in my own mind, whether I shall add anything in my feeble way to the hopes, the prayers, the aspirations, that are going forth daily for the perpetuity of the Union of these States. I ask myself, shall I add anything to that volume of invocation which is everywhere rising up to high Heaven, ' *Spare us from the madness of disunion and civil war !'*

" Sir, standing in this Chamber, and speaking on this subject, I cannot forget that I am standing in a place once occupied by one far mightier than I, the latchet of whose shoes I am not worthy to unloose. It was upon this subject of secession, of disunion, of discord, of civil war, that Mr. Webster uttered those immortal sentiments, clothed in immortal words, married to the noblest expressions that ever fell from

7

human lips; which alone would have made him memorable, and
remembered forever. Sir, I cannot improve upon those expressions.
They were uttered nearly thirty years ago, in the face of what was
imagined to be a great danger, then happily dissipated. They were
uttered in the fullness of his genius, from the fullness of his heart.
They have found an echo since then in millions of homes, and in
foreign lands. They have been a text book in schools. They have
been an inspiration to public hope and to public liberty. As I close, I
repeat them. If, in their presence, I were to attempt to give utterance
to any words of my own, I should feel that I ought to say,

> "And shall the Lyre, so long divine,
> Degenerate into hands like mine?"

" Sir, I adopt the closing passages of that immortal speech; they
are my sentiments; they are the sentiments of every man on this side
of the Chamber. I would fain believe they are the sentiments of
every man on this floor. I would fain believe they were an inspiration,
and will become a power throughout the length and breadth of this
Confederacy—that again the aspirations, and hopes, and prayers for
the Union, may rise like a perpetual hymn of praise. But, sir, however this may be, these thoughts are mine, these prayers are mine,
and as reverently and fondly I utter them, I leave the discussion:

" ' When my eyes shall be turned to behold for the last time, the sun
in heaven, may I not see him shining on the broken and dishonored
fragments of a once glorious Union; on States dissevered, discordant,
belligerent; on a land rent with civil feuds, or drenched, it may be, in
fraternal blood! Let their last feeble, lingering glance rather
behold the gorgeous ensign of the Republic, now known and honored
throughout the earth, still full high advanced, its arms and trophies
streaming in their original lustre; not a stripe erased nor polluted, not
a single star obscured, bearing for its motto no such miserable inter-
rogatory as 'What is all this worth?' Nor those other words of
delusion and folly, 'Liberty first, and Union afterwards;' but everywhere, spread all over in characters of living light, blazing on all its
ample folds as they float over the sea, and over the land, and in every
wind under the whole heavens, that other sentiment, dear to every

true American heart, Liberty and Union, now and forever, one and inseparable.' "

In this highly ornate, as well as logical speech, and, we may add, in all of his public utterances, Senator Baker reminds us of what Plutarch so inimitably says of Pericles : That, " desirous to make his language a proper vehicle for his sublime sentiments, and to speak in a manner that became the dignity of his life, he availed himself greatly of what he had learned of Anxagoras, adorning his eloquence with the rich colors of philosophy ; for, adding the loftiness of imagination, and all-commanding energy, with which philosophy supplied him, to his native powers of genius, and making use of whatever he found to his purpose in the study of nature to dignify the art of speaking, he far excelled all other orators."

REMARKS ON THE PACIFIC RAILROAD BILL.

On January 5th, 1861, the Senate, in Committee of the Whole, having under consideration the bill to secure contracts, and make provision for the safe, certain and more speedy transportation by railroad, of mails, troops and munitions of war, between the Atlantic States and those of the Pacific, and for other purposes, Mr. Baker made a forcible speech in favor of the bill, from which we collate the following interesting passages :

" I had been led to suppose, when I came here, that there was a party in Congress, in favor of a Pacific Railroad. I believe I am mistaken ; or if there be, I am sure it is lying supinely by, and giving control of the supposed measure into the hands of its enemies. We have seen every conceivable mode of objection, which the time will permit, made against it, with the appearance sometimes of friendship, but with all the tenacity of enmity. Gentlemen forget, in their objections, whatever may be learned from experience as to legislation upon subjects somewhat kindred. Now, I understand the distinguished Senator from Mississippi, (Mr. Davis) who has just spoken, to say, that he will not go for any measure which will give the Government political control, and that he will not go for any measure which will tend to enrich individuals. * * * That line of objection which attacks a measure, because the Government may have too much to do with it, and because individuals may have too much to do with it, will leave it between two stools and let it fall to the ground.

"One gentleman objects that he will not make a grant of land to anybody, for any thing, except subject to the condition that Congress shall supervise State legislation, and approve the acts of incorporation that individuals may get of the State governments. All that class of objections are, I will not say intended, but framed, to defeat the road. Now, after ten years struggle ; after hope so long deferred ; when the Representatives of the people by a very large majority, after every conceivable objection has been made and answered ; when the condition of public affairs ; when a desire to end sectional strife ; when a desire for the Union ; when every reason so well presented by the distinguished Senator from New York, would seem to point out to us the necessity of doing it at once, it appears to me that we are further off from it to-day than ever. And the reason why, it strikes me, that we are further than usual ,is this: that objections which have been answered in every State Legislature, on every incorporation bill from the time legislation commenced on such subjects, seem to weigh with unwonted force on the minds of a large majority of this body.

"Take the sectional objection offered by my distinguished friend from Louisiana ; and I attempt to answer these objections, briefly. The gentleman says—looking at the sectional aspect of the subject— 'here are fifty-three individuals, your corporators, from fourteen States.' Now, sir, this bill proposes two roads, and not one ; two sets of corporators and not one ; and, I think, the gentleman, in fairness, ought to have stated that fact in conjunction with what he has said.

It is true that the corporators for one road are selected from fourteen States of the Union; but it is also true, as I am informed, that the grant which is made to the persons who are to be incorporated to make the second road—the Texas road—inures really to persons all over the southern portion of the Union. And, if gentlemen had paid the attention to this subject they do to most others, I think they would have learned that, from the history of its passage through the other House, and would have accommodated their views to that fact.

"But, again, sir, every one knows that the history of making railroads in this country, is an attempt upon the part of the Government, where they do give advantage to somebody, to combine individual skill, effort and caution, with Government authority and money. That is the use of a bill incorporating individuals, and has been from the beginning. If, according to the plan suggested by the gentleman from Mississippi, the Government alone were to do it, we have always been told that Government would spend its money in the most wasteful and ineffective way in the world. Therefore, the usual course has been to unite the skill and care of individuals in the Government expenditures. This bill endeavors to do that. It follows out the plan that States adopt, and, I believe, the plan that Congress has often adopted before. It adopts the plan upon which the great railroads of Illinois have been built—a plan, which, in my judgment, has proved itself more successful than any other upon which a Government has ever attempted to complete a great work for the benefit of its people. * * *
* * * "I am for one road. If I do not understand this measure, at least I have thought of it; I know what my people desire. If I had my way, I would say, unhesitatingly, make a road from San Francisco as near to St. Louis as you can get it. It appears to me, that every consideration would point out that as the best way. Again: I am an old Whig; I am not afraid of extending the power of this Government; I wish it was a more consolidated and stronger government than it is; I have not a bit of respect for this idea of State's rights, which is now convulsing this country to its center; and if I had my choice, I would build the road with the power of the Government, with the money of the Government, for the benefit of the people, and I would build it at

any cost.   But I cannot have my way ; I am obliged to concede, to compromise.   Accordingly, I meet the Senator from California, with whom it is my fortune to agree about hardly anything, and I adapt myself, as far as I can, to his plan ; and he in turn, conforms himself to the opinions of various other distinguished gentlemen on this floor ; not getting that which he would desire, but getting the best he can ; harmonizing all interests and settling all conflicts.   Sir, is not that statesmanlike ?   Is any great measure ever adopted otherwise, either in Government or in administration ?   Was not the Constitution so formed ?   And to say to us, ' we will not go for the greatest measure of the age, or of the world, because it does not begin exactly at the right spot, because the money is not spent exactly by the right man, because it does not end exactly in the right place,' would be to divide us into endless fractions of opinion, never being able to arrive at a sensible result.   Therefore, it is that I appeal, not to the enemies of the bill, but to its friends—men who have advocated it in the country, in discussion before the people ; men who come here to reflect the true opinion of their States—I ask them now, in the time of its trial, to give up mere questions of locality, to give up objections as to this man or the other, and agree with what the deliberate wisdom of the popular branch, after three years effort, has determined to be practical.   *   *
   *   *   *   *   *   *   "I have but one other word, and I close. I, like my friend from California, feel that interest in the passage of this bill which belongs to our Western coast.   We are very far off ; we are loyal to the Union ; we will remain with it, whether you give us this road or not ; but almost everything in which a government can assist or protect a people, is connected with the passage of this bill. Its enemies know very well, and the distinguished gentleman who has led its defense so long, knows it still better than they, that if you amend this bill now, in any important particular, you defeat it for this session, and probably forever.   My distinguished friend from Louisiana knows well that that is so, when he attacks it with his acuteness and vigor ; I think the gentleman from Mississippi knows that very well, when he presents an attack not so acute, but broad, comprehensive, general—none the less fierce.   And it astonishes me, that we Republicans, for ten years the advocates of the great general idea ; for ten

years holding out the hope which we have learned from the people themselves; that we, now, when we have the power, when we have kind and generous friends, not named as Republicans, with us, whose interests or whose patriotism lead them to act with us, enough to carry the bill; that we, dividing upon minor points, should let the bill go by, and cling from mere pride and petty objection to that line of policy which must insure its entire, perhaps permanent defeat."

Again, on January 15th, when the Senate, in Committee of the Whole, resumed the consideration of the Pacific Railroad bill, Mr. Baker addressed the Committee, briefly, as follows:

"Mr. President, what has been said in relation to this *northern* road compels me, reluctantly, to say a very few words, which I trust my friends here, and, indeed, on both sides of the Chamber, will attend to. I am going to vote for the bill as it is, as nearly as I can, without any amendments or alterations; and I am going to do so, while, as I believe, I represent a constituency further north than any other gentleman upon this floor. I am going to vote against any material amendment, or any at all, although I am told that the northern route, proposed, will benefit the immediate people whom I represent, very greatly. While I do so, I know that I shall be misapprehended—I will not say misrepresented—at home. I know the argument will bear upon me as heavily as it can bear upon any gentleman on this side of the Chamber, who may vote as I do, that I am not voting for the immediate interests of my constituents, by bringing the road nearer their homes and through their farms. I must meet that as I may.

"I desire to say here, and to give it as much publicity as I can, just this: having lived for ten years on the Pacific coast, where our whole hopes have been directed towards some road, I see at last a prospect of accomplishing that result by this bill. I have observed, with great care, the struggle in the other House; and I have seen that, by an overwhelming vote, the proposition for a northern route has been defeated. I am sure—and I take the advice of all the original friends of the bill around me—that to incorporate any amendment in the bill now, will defeat it for this session, and possibly forever. In that condition, quite alive to the interests of my constituents, quite sure that my conduct may be the subject of misapprehension or misrepresentation, quite sure that all that strong feeling of locality for our State, our road, may be brought to bear upon me in future; yet, risking my justification upon the great idea that I believe I am doing the best I can to promote the connection between the Atlantic and the Pacific, now, I shall vote for these roads; and, if hereafter, my vote may ever be brought in question. I have but this to say: no man who can observe the condition in which this bill is to-day in the Senate, can do otherwise than know, that unless we do, within a very few days, pass the measure, substantially as it is, we cannot pass it this session, and we risk it forever.

"The bill, in my judgment, is far from perfect. As an original bill, I think—as I have said before—there ought to be but *one* road, one great highway of nations and of empires; not for one Government, nor for one day, nor for one generation, but for all the world, and all the advancing generations who may partake of its benefits and its blessings. But, in an age of compromise, and in a Government of compromise, I find that we have, after ten years, accommodated ourselves to each others opinions; so that now, with two roads, we may pass a bill, may get it through this body, and it may receive the sanction of the President of the United States. Shall I, can I, dare I risk the measure to which the hopes, the prayers, the aspirations of so many thousands, distant very far from here, have been directed so long? And with all humility, without offering my own example for other people to follow at all, I hope I may say to my friends on this side of Chamber: Gentlemen, if the road does not suit you in its locality, if you want one more or one less, let me beseech you to take this now, lest, indeed, we lose all."

Mr. Baker was a firm friend and advocate of the Pacific Railroad project, from its inception, and to attain that much desired end, he was willing to sacrifice any personal preference for a particular route, though such an one might have been more acceptable to his immediate constituents. He had assisted in building the Panama Railroad; had witnessed its complete success, exceeding the highest anticipations of its projectors; and he foresaw with the eye of a seer, that the spanning of the continent with a belt of iron, from New York to San Francisco, would not only strengthen the bonds of the Union, but revolutionize to a considerable extent the commerce of the world, and bring the rich treasures of the Orient directly to our doors. Could he have lived until the present day, when this prodigious enterprise is a *fait accompli*, and been present at the recent memorable celebration of its completion—and no one would have enjoyed the occasion more than himself— he would likely have made a speech which would have entirely eclipsed all his former efforts in the way of oratory, and outshone others, as does the "golden spike," which lifts its glittering head beneath the shadow of the Sierra Nevada, outshine its fellows.

During the same session, Senator Baker made remarks, more or less extended, on the Army Bill, the Tariff Bill, and the bill for expenses incurred in our hostilities with the Indians in Oregon. He also, on March 1st, 1861, delivered a pertinent and convincing speech in support of the joint resolutions proposing amendments to the Constitution of the United States, known as the

PEACE CONFERENCE PROPOSITIONS,

In the hope that their adoption by Congress, and submission to the people of the several States for ratification,

8

would tend to restore peace to a distracted country. The plan of our work will not permit the introduction of the whole of this speech; but the subjoined copious extracts may serve to illustrate its general style, tone, and mode of treatment of the complicated and perplexing questions at issue between the two sections of the Confederacy:

" Mr. President, I mean to vote for the passage of these proposed amendments just as they are, without any change ; and I propose to give, very briefly, a few of the reasons which govern my judgment in the act.

" In the first place, I feel that I am submitting to the people of the whole country, amendments which they, and they only, can incorporate into the present Constitution ; and I do not believe that, in any state of the case, I can do very wrong in doing that; but when I consider the immediate condition of the country, I feel that I am doing very right. Twenty States assemble in what is called the peace convention. They recommend to us, in times of great trial and difficulty, the passage of these resolutions. They are eminent men ; they are—very many of them—great men; they have been selected by the States which they represent, because of their purity of character and ability. The country is in great trouble. Six States have seceded ; and I am told by many men, in whom I have great confidence, that their States are to-day trembling in the balance. I believe it. I am told—but upon that subject I have not yet made up my mind—that the adoption of these measures by the people will heal the differences with the border States. I do not believe that I can do wrong, therefore, in giving the people of the whole Union a chance to determine these questions.

" In the beginning, I voted against the propositions of the distinguished Senator from Kentucky. (Mr. Crittenden.) Even then, I did not perceive any great harm in submitting any propositions to the people of the United States, which circumstances might appear to render necessary for any good purpose. I refused to vote for them for two reasons: first, I believed something better might be attained; and second, I did not believe that the people of the States would agree to them. I do not believe it now, and for one simple reason: I think I may consider myself, in some respects, a representative of the opinion as well as the power of my own people. I am a Republican, a zealous and determined one. I have all my life been of the opinion that Congress ought not to protect slavery, and to extend the dominion of this Government for that purpose, or with that possibility. A great many in the North, who are not Republicans, but are what we call Douglas men, have shown at the last election, under something of trial and sacrifice, that they too, do not believe that the Constitution does, or ought to extend slavery. I am not disposed to give up that opinion; I do not believe they are. I was not disposed to give up when six States were in the Union, which are now out, as they say; and I am not disposed to give it up yet. Independently of pride of opinion, I do not believe that kind of sacrifice would acomplish any good result.

"These are the reasons, in short, which induced me to vote, with regret, against the propositions of the distinguished Senator from Kentucky in the earlier part of the session. But now, we are within two days of adjournment, propositions essentially variant in their character to those, are submitted here; and I am asked: 'will you, in your representative capacity, submit these to your people for their decision, either to accept or reject?' Now, why not? I need not dwell upon the fact that, while we are a representative, we are at the same time a democratic Government. I will not shut my eyes to the fact, that, though the Republican party is in a constitutional majority, it is not yet, and it never has been, in an actual majority; and I do not believe it possible for one third of the people to coerce the opinion of two thirds. * * *

Mr. WILKINSON. "I understood the Senator to say that twenty States appealed to us.

Mr. BAKER. "Yes, sir, just as I say the Government appeals to another Government. I do not say every individual in it; just as I say Congress appeals to another Government, not every individual member of Congress; but I do say, in the words of the proposition

before us, that 'they', the Peace Convention, composed of the States
recited, 'have approved what is herewith recited, and respectfully
request that your honorable body will submit it to conventions in the
States, as article thirteen of the amendments to the Constitution of
the United States.' That is all I said, or meant to say.

"Now, sir, suppose that every argument that the distinguished
Senators from Virginia have brought to bear on this proposition is
true, what then? Is that any reason why it should not be submitted
to the people? Suppose they do not approve of it, what then? It is
their business, not ours. And suppose they should, it is a measure of
peace, of security, of union. Sir, I know, as you do, many of the
members of that Convention. I have acted with them as Whigs in
old times, and I wish they could come back. I know that they have
proved in former times, as they will prove again, that they love this
Union to the very depth and core of their hearts. I do not propose
to give them up; I do not propose to weaken them; I do admire, with
my whole heart, the sacrifice of opinion which they make, and which
is typified by the noble expression of the distinguished Senator from
Kentucky to-day. Party or no party, North or no North, I, at least,
will meet them half way. My State is far distant. She had no
members in that Convention. I do not know whether she will approve
this measure; but I know it will neither hurt that State nor me, to
give her a chance to determine. I know very well that the Senators
from Virginia do not approve it. That is the reason why I do.
(Laughter.) If I was sure they would not think me guilty of disrespect,
I would remind them of what was said by a distinguished man in old
times. Phocian, in the last days of his Republic—and I hope in that
respect, at least, there will be no parallel—Phocian was once making
a speech to the Athenian people, and something he said excited very
great applause. He turned around to the friends near him, and
remarked: 'what foolish thing have I been saying that these people
praise me?' Sir, if Virginia, represented as she is here to-day, and as
she has been during this session—not as I think she *really* is—were to
approve these propositions, I should doubt them very much indeed.

*   *   *   *   *   *   *   *   *   *   *

"Mr. President, let us be just to these propositions. As a

Republican, I give up something when I vote for them; but, sir, I am not voting for them now; I am only voting to submit them to my people; and I shall go before them, when the time comes, being governed in my own opinion as to whether they should vote for them or not, as I see that Virginia, Tennessee, Kentucky, North Carolina and Missouri, by their people, desire. To be frank, sir, if this proposition will suit the Border States, if there will be peace, and union, and loyalty and brotherhood, with this, I will vote for it at the polls, with all my heart and soul; but if I see that the counsels of the Senators from Virginia shall prevail; if my noble friend from Tennessee (Mr. Johnson) shall be overwhelmed; if secession shall still grow in the public mind there; if they are determined, upon artificial causes of complaint, as I believe, still to unite their fate, their destiny, their hope, with the extremest South, then, perceiving them to be of no avail, I shall refuse them. Therefore, at the polls at last, I shall be governed as an individual citizen by my conviction at the moment of what the ultimate result of these propositions will be—but I am not voting for that to-day. I am saying: 'People of the United States, I submit it to you; twenty States demand it; the peace of the country requires it; there is dissolution in the atmosphere; States have gone off; others threaten; the Queen of England upon her throne declares to the whole world her sympathy with our unfortunate condition; foreign Governments denote that there is danger, to-day, that the greatest Confederation the world has ever seen is to be parted in pieces, never to be united.' Now, not what I wish, not what I want, not what I would have, but all that I can get, is before me. If the people of Oregon do not like it, they can easily reject it. If the people of Pennsylvania will not have it, they can easily throw it aside. If they do not believe there is danger of dissolution, if they prefer dissolution, if they think they can compel fifteen States to remain in, or come back, or if they believe they will not go out, let them reject it. I repeat again, it is their business, not mine.

"But, sir, whether I vote for it or not, in voting for it here, it may be said that I give up some of my principles. Mr. President, we sometimes mistake our opinions for our principles. I am appealed to often—it is said to me: 'you believed' in the Chicago platform.' Suppose I did. 'Well, this varies from the Chicago platform.' Suppose it does. I stand to-day, as I believe, in the presence of greater events than those which attend the making of a President. I stand, as I believe, in the presence of peace and war, and if it were true that I did violate the Chicago platform, the Chicago platform is not the Constitution of the United States to me. If events, if circumstances change, I will violate it, appealing to my conscience, to my country, and to my God, to justify me according to the motive.

"Again, sir, how much do I give up? I have said, as a Republican, that Congress has the power to prohibit slavery in all the Territories of the United States. I believe it to-day. Talking about giving up, there are a good many other people that give up something here. Gentlemen on the other side, who have been contending that Congress had no power whatever to prohibit slavery, acknowledge that they were mistaken; at any rate they go for it; they prohibit it by law, by the Constitution itself. Therefore, I am not the only man who gives up.

"Again: I believe it is wrong, politically wrong—I am not now discussing the social and moral question—to establish slavery in the name of freedom. Sir, twelve years ago, or more, it was my fortune to wander in a foreign land, beneath the stars and stripes of my country. I went there, as I think, impelled by motives of patriotism, perhaps having mingled with them not a little desire of adventure, love of change, and that feverish excitement for which we people of this country are always and everywhere remarkable; but I believe that I did suppose I was doing something to repay the country for much she had done for me. Sir, often and again, wandering sometimes beneath

'Where Orizaba's purpled summit shone,'

sometimes by the dark pestilential river that marks the boundary between the two countries, often and often have I wondered by myself whether I was wandering and suffering there to spread slavery over an unwilling people. I am not sorry to see that now that is rendered impossible; first, in the course of events; but if it were not so, I know, if these propositions shall pass, that the foul blot of slavery never will be extended over one foot of Territory to be taken or conquered by the people of the United States.

" But, I am asked, 'what do you say about New Mexico?' I will tell you in twenty words. I am an older Republican than many of those I see around me, who vote to-day differently from me. I voted, in 1850, on the floor of the other House, against the compromise measures of that year. I did so, among other reasons, because I was not willing that Utah and New Mexico should become slave or free according to the wishes of their people, believing as I did, (I have changed my opinion in some respects since) that that was not best for the whole country. Contrary to my wishes, those compromise measures prevailed. New Mexico now is nominally a slave Territory; that is, to use the words of the distinguished Senator from New York, (Mr. Seward) there are some twenty slaves in the whole Territory. There they may, probably will, remain. I submit to the people a proposition, that if they approve it as a compromise, as a concession, for peace and union, as it happens that that little Territory includes all that can possibly be slave territory, they will let it alone until the people are able and willing to make their own State Constitution.

* * * * * * * * * * * *

" Again, It is said on the Republican side, that we protect slavery. In one sense we do, and in another we do not. When the resolutions of the Senator from Kentucky were up the other day, I voted for the amendment of the other Senator from Kentucky (Mr. Powell) in order to make them clear, to show what I was voting against. I was unwilling that territory, hereafter to be acquired, should be rendered slave territory; and I put that proposition distinctly in it, so that when I voted against them, it might be seen how and why I did it. As I have said, this proposition renders that impossible. First, it refers only to the territory we now possess—that is New Mexico alone. As for the territory north of 36 30, I need not speak. We know that God Almighty has registered a decree that that shall never be slave. We, on our part, want no Wilmot Proviso there; we all agree that we are willing to let it alone. South, there is the barren Territory of New Mexico. Beyond that, who knows? If we are to acquire it, we are to acquire it by this proposition, by the assent of a majority of the States of both sections, and two thirds of the whole; and I do not know a man living who believes that, with that prohibition incorporated in the Constitution, slavery is probable, or even possible.

"Therefore, Mr. President, I agree that in the compromise, I, as a Republican, do give up to that extent, and no more, what I have said; but doing that, I believe that I consecrate all the territory between here and Cape Horn, to freedom, with all its blessings forever.

*   *   *   *   *   *   *   *   *   *   *

Mr. President, I should be excessively pleased, as a partisan and a man, if the inauguration of Mr. Lincoln could be one at which all the States would attend with the old good feeling, and the old good humor. I have seen six States separate themselves, as they say, from us, and form a new confederacy, with great pain and greater surprise. I cannot shut my eyes, if I would, to the existing state of things. I listen to the warning of my friend, from Tennessee. I have been in both States. I know something of their people. I believe that there, even there, the Union is in danger; and I believe if we break up here without some attempt to reconcile them to us, and us to them, many of the predictions of friends and foes as to the danger will be accomplished. I said in the earlier part of the session—I repeat it—I will yield nothing to secession. When the Representatives from South Carolina, Alabama and Louisiana, came here invoking war, telling us that if we did not yield to them, they would secede, would break up the Union, would confederate with foreign governments, would hold us as aliens and strangers and enemies, I believed then, as I believe now, that that was too dear a price to pay even for union and peace; but to-day the case is altered. Virginia, Kentucky, Tennessee, reiterate their love for the Union. They tell us in unmistakable terms that they desire to remain; and in every county, nay, in every township of those States, we have staunch and true and ardent friends, who would be willing to seal their devotion to this Union with their blood. It is *they* to whose appeal I would listen. It is from them that I would take counsel and advice; and when they tell me, 'pass these resolutions; they are resolutions of peace; submit them to your people; listen to what ours say in reply; if it appears to you at the polls that these resolutions will produce peace, restore the Union, create or renew fraternal feeling, pass them; let us settle this question, and be one people,' I agree with all my heart, I will do it.

*   *   *   *   *   *   *   *   *   *   *

"Besides, sir, what else can I do? As I sit down let me ask Senators on every side, what else can any of us do? Shall we sit here for three months, when petition, resolution, acclamation, tumult is heard, seen, and felt on every side, and do nothing? Shall State after State go out, and not warn us of danger? Shall Senators, Representatives, patriotic, eloquent, venerable, tell us again and again of danger in their States, and we condescend to make no reply?"

On the day succeeding the delivery of the foregoing speech, when, in a debate in the Senate on the same subject, Mr. Baker's position was assailed by Senator Trumbull, and other Republican Senators, he replied with becoming spirit, and in the course of his remarks used the following pointed language:

"Mr. President: In the earlier days of the session, I seized what was rather a remarkable occasion to say, that, in my judgment, secession had no warrant in the Constitution, that it was disorganizing and destructive. I said so then, and believe it still; and sir, if I may add my sentiments to my conviction, I may say further, if that time shall come, when, in the judgment of the whole country, under the auspices of a new Administration, in the presence of the world, it shall be necessary for the peace of the Union, and for the preservation of the great principles of free government, to put down secession by force, I will not be behind those who profess themselves willing to lead the advance now. But, sir, I am so fearful of the effect of the secession of seven States, that I do want, in my heart, to avoid the secession of fifteen."

The propositions of the Peace Conference, it is known, were strenuously opposed by the extreme men in Congress from both sections of the Union, and the measure consequently failed, as, in like manner, did the "Border State," and the "Crittenden—Douglas Compromise."

It should be remembered to Baker's honor as a public man, that, during this most troubled and momentous

9

session of the National Legislature, he was one of the few Senators of the dominant party, who seemed to fully comprehend the magnitude of the issues presented, to appreciate the dangers which beset the Republic, and who manifested a hearty willingness to meet the great crisis in a spirit of liberality, conciliation, and wise statesmanship, which, had it been more generally imitated and sustained, might have led to a very different result from that of a protracted and ruinous internecine war.

And yet, when a little later, the portentous storm of war, which had long been gathering in the southern horizon, burst upon the land in all its fury, he hesitated not as to the course he should pursue ; but buckled on his armor, and nerved himself to engage in the terrible and bloody strife.

HE SPEAKS IN NEW YORK CITY—ENTERS THE FIELD IN THE WAR OF THE REBELLION.

On the 20th of April—a few days after the fall of Fort Sumter—while the cry to arms was being echoed and re-echoed from the Capital to the utmost limit of the Confederacy, Colonel Baker spoke in Union Park, New York City, to one of the largest assemblages ever enchained by the eloquence of a single man. In closing his stirring address, he dedicated himself anew to the service of his country in these grandly eloquent words, which were greeted with tremendous applause :

"And if, from the far Pacific, a voice, feebler than the " feeblest murmur on its shore, may be heard to give

"you courage and hope in this contest, that voice is
"yours to-day. And if a man, whose hair is gray, who
"is well nigh worn out in the battle and toil of life,
"may pledge himself on such an occasion, and to such
"an audience, let me say, as my last word : that as when,
"amid sheeted fire and flame, I saw and led the hosts
"of New York, as they charged in contest upon a
"foreign soil for the honor of your flag; so, again, if
"Providence shall will it, this feeble hand shall draw a
"sword, never yet dishonored—not to fight for distant
"honor in a foreign land—but to fight for country, for
"government, for constitution, for law, for right, for
"freedom, for humanity; and in the hope that the
"banner of our country may advance, and whersoever
"that banner waves, there may glory pursue and free-
"dom be established."

Unlike some of our modern school of patriots, Baker
was a man of ACTION as well as of words. He at once
commenced work in earnest, by recruiting, in Philadelphia and vicinity, what was called his "California
Regiment;" which being soon filled to the maximum
number was accepted by the Government, and mustered
into service. President Lincoln, about this time, tendered
him a Brigadier General's commission, but he declined
the proffered honor, probably because it would have
vacated his seat in the Senate.

HIS MEMORABLE REPLY TO SENATOR BRECKENRIDGE.

At the first session of the 37th Congress, convoked
by proclamation of the President on July 4th, 1861,

Senator Baker was in his seat, and participated prominently in the passage of those important measures which became necessary to place the nation upon a war footing.

During this session, pending the debate in the Senate on the "Insurrection and Sedition bill," he made his famous impromptu reply to Senator John C. Breckenridge, of Kentucky. This speech created a very marked sensation at the time, and is thought by some to have been the happiest effort of his life. It is, indeed, a most admirable specimen of impassioned declamation, and merits scrutiny as a model of its class. After addressing himself first, to the merits of the bill in question, he spoke as follows:

"I agree that we ought to do all we can to limit, to restrain, to fetter the abuse of military power. Bayonets are at best illogical arguments. I am not willing, except as a case of sheerest necessity, ever to permit a military commander to exercise authority over life, liberty and property. But, sir, it is part of the law of war; you cannot organize juries; you cannot have trials according to the forms and ceremonials of the common law amid the clangor of arms; and somebody must enforce police regulations in a conquered or occupied district. I ask the Senator from Kentucky again, respectfully, is that unconstitutional; or if in the nature of war it must exist, even if there be no law passed by us to allow it, is it unconstitutional to allow it? That is the question, to which I do not think he will make a clear and distinct reply.

"Now, sir, I have shown him two sections of the bill, which I do not think he will repeat earnestly are unconstitutional. I do not think he will seriously deny that it is perfectly constitutional to limit, to regulate, to control, and at the same time to confer and restrain authority in the hands of military commanders. I think it is wise and judicious to regulate it by virtue of powers to be placed in the hands of the President, by law.

" Now, a few words in reference to the Senator's predictions. The Senator from Kentucky stands up here in a manly way, in opposition to what he sees is the overwhelming sentiment of the Senate, and utters malediction and prediction combined. Well, sir, it is not every prediction that is prophecy. It is the easiest thing in the world to do ; there is nothing easier, except to be mistaken when we have predicted. I confess, Mr. President, that I would not have predicted three weeks ago the disasters which have overtaken our arms, and I do not think that, six months hence, the Senator will indulge in the same prediction which is his favorite key now. I would ask him what would you have us do ? A Confederate army within twenty miles of us, advancing, or threatening to advance to overwhelm your Government, to shake the pillars of the Union, to bring them around your head, if you stay here. Are we to stop and talk about an uprising of the popular sentiment in the North against the war ? Are we to predict evil, and then retire from what we predict ? Is it not the more manly part to go on as we have begun, to raise money, and levy armies, to organize them, and prepare to advance, by all the laws and regulations that civilization and humanity allow in time of war ? Can we do anything more ? To talk about stopping is idle ; we will never stop. Will the Senator yield to rebellion ? Will he shrink from armed insurrection ? Will his State justify it ? Will its better public sentiment allow it ? Shall we send a flag of truce ? What would he have us do ? Or would he conduct this war so feebly that the whole world would smile at us in derision ?

" These speeches of his, thrown broadcast over the land, what clear, distinct meaning have they ? Are they not intended to animate our enemies ? Sir, are they not words of brilliant, polished treason, even in the Capitol of our Confederacy ? What would have been thought, if in another Capital, in another Republic, and in a yet more martial age, a Senator as grave, not more eloquent or dignified than the Senator from Kentucky, yet with the Roman purple flowing over his shoulders, had risen from his place, surrounded by all the illustrations of Roman glory, and declared that advancing Hannibal was just, and that Carthage should be dealt with in terms of mercy? What would have been thought, if after the battle of Cannæ, a Senator had then risen in his place, and denounced every levy of the Roman people, every expenditure of its treasure, and every appeal to old recollections and old glories? Sir, a Senator, *himself far more learned in such lore, tells me in a voice I am glad is audible, that he would have been hurled from the Tarpeian Rock. It is a grand commentary on the American Constitution that we permit these words to be uttered.

"I ask the Senator to recollect to what, save to send aid and comfort to the enemy, do these predictions of his amount to? Every word thus uttered fall as a note of inspiration upon every Confederate ear. Every sound thus uttered is a word (and falling from his lips, a mighty word) of kindling and triumph, to a foe that is determined to advance. For me, I have no such words as the Senator, to utter. For me, amid temporary defeat, disaster and disgrace, it seems that my duty calls me to utter another word, and that word is bold, sudden, forward, determined war, according to the laws of war—by armies, by military commanders, clothed with full power, advancing with all the past glories of the Republic urging them on to conquest.

"I do not stop to consider whether it is subjugation or not. It is compulsory obedience; not to my will, not to yours, sir; not to the will of any one man; not to the will of any one State; but compulsory obedience to the Constitution of the whole country. The Senator chose the other day, again and again, to animadvert on a single expression in a little speech which I delivered before the Senate, in which I took occasion to say, that if the people of the rebellious States would not govern themselves as States, they ought to be governed as Territories. The Senator knew full well, for I explained it twice, that on this side of the Chamber, nay, in this whole Chamber; nay, in the whole North and West; nay, in all the Loyal States, in all their length and breadth, there is not a man among us all who dreams of causing any man in the South to submit to any rule, either as to life, liberty or property, that we ourselves do not willingly agree to yield to. Did he ever think of that? When we

---

* The late Wm. P. Fessenden.

subjugate South Carolina, what shall we do? We shall compel obedience to the Constitution of the United States; that is all. We do not mean, we have never said, any more. If it be slavery that men should obey the Constitution their fathers fought for, let it be so. If it be freedom, it is freedom equally for them and us. We propose to subjugate rebellion into loyalty; we propose to subjugate insurrection into peace; we propose to subjugate Confederate anarchy into Constitutional Union liberty. The Senator well knows that we propose no more. I ask him, I appeal to his better judgment now; what does he imagine we intend to do, if, fortunately, we conquer Tennessee or South Carolina—call it 'conquer' if you will. Sir, what do we propose to do? They will have their courts still; they will have their ballot boxes still; they will have their elections still; they will have their representatives upon this floor still; they will have the writ of Habeas Corpus still; they will have every privilege they ever had, and all we desire. When the Confederate armies are scattered; when their leaders are banished from power; when the people return to a late repentent sense of the wrong they have done to a Government they never felt but in benignancy and blessing, then the Constitution, made for all, will be felt by all alike, like the descending rains from heaven, which bless all alike. Is that subjugation? To restore what was for the benefit of the whole country, and of the whole human race, is all we desire, and all we can have.

"Gentlemen talk about the North-east. I appeal to Senators from the North-east: is there a man in all your States, who advances upon the South with any other idea but to restore the Constitution of the United States in its spirit and in its unity? I never heard that one. I believe that no man indulges in any dream of inflicting there any wrong to public liberty, and I respectfully tell the Senator from Kentucky that he persistently, earnestly, I will not say willfully, misrepresents the sentiment of the North and West, when he attempts to teach these doctrines to the confederates of the South.

"Sir, while I am predicting, I will tell you another thing. This threat about money and men amounts to nothing. Some of the States which have been named in that connection, I know will. I know, as my friend from Illinois will bear me witness, his own State very well.

I am sure that no temporary defeat, no momentary disgrace, will swerve that State either from its allegiance to the Union, or from its determination to preserve it. It is not with us a question of money or of blood; it is a question involving considerations higher than these. When the Senator from Kentucky speaks of the Pacific, I see another distinguished friend from Illinois, now worthily representing one of the States on the Pacific, (Mr. McDougall) who will bear me witness that I know that State, too, well. I take the liberty—I know I but utter his sentiments in advance—joining with him, to say, that that State (quoting from the passage the gentleman himself has quoted,) will be true to the Union to the last of her blood and treasure. There may be there some disaffected; there may be some few men there, who would rather ' rule in hell than serve in heaven.' There are such men everywhere. There are a few men there, who have left the South for the good of the South; who are perverse, violent, destructive, revolutionary, and opposed to social order. A few, but very few, thus formed and thus nurtured, in California and in Oregon, both persistently endeavoring to create and maintain mischief; but the great portion of our population are loyal to the core, and in every chord of their hearts. They are offering through me—more to their own Senators every day, from California and, indeed, from Oregon—to add to the legions of this country by the hundred and the thousand. They are willing to come thousands of miles with their arms on their shoulders, at their own expense, to share with the offering of their hearts blood in the great struggle for constitutional liberty. I tell the Senator that his predictions, sometimes for the South, sometimes for the Middle States, sometimes for the North-east, and then wandering in airy visions out to the far Pacific, about the dread of our people as for loss of blood and treasure, provoking them to disloyalty, are false in fact, and false in theory. The Senator from Kentucky is mistaken in them all. Five hundred million dollars! What then? Great Britian gave more than two thousand millions in the great battle for constitutianal liberty which she led, at one time, almost single handed against the world. Five hundred thousand men! What then? We have them; they are the children of the country. They belong to the whole country; they are our sons, our kinsmen; and there are many of us who will give them all up before we will abate one word of our just demand, or will retreat one inch from the line which divides right from wrong.

"Sir, it is not a question of men or money. All the money, all the men, are, in our judgment, well bestowed in such a cause. When we give them, we know their value well; we give them with the more pride and joy. Sir, how can we retreat? Sir, how can we make peace? Who will treat? What Commissioners? Who go? Upon what terms? Where is to be your boundary line? Where the end of the principles we shall have to give up? What will become of constitutional government? What will become of past glories? What of future hopes? Shall we sink into the insignificance of the grave, a degraded, defeated, emasculated people—frightened by the results of one battle, and scared by the visions raised by the imagination of the Senator from Kentucky upon this floor. No, sir, a thousand times no. We will rally, if, indeed, our words be necessary; we will rally the people, the loyal people of the country. They will pour forth their treasures, their money, their men, without stint and without measure. The most peaceful man in this body may stamp his foot upon this Senate floor, as of old a warrior and Senator did, and from that single stamp there will spring forth armed legions. Shall one battle, or a dozen battles, determine the fate of an empire—the loss of one thousand men or twenty thousand men—the expenditure of $100,000,000 or $500,000,000. In a year peace, in ten years at most of peaceful progress, we can restore them all.

"There will be some graves reeking with blood, watered by the tears of affection. There will be some privation; there will be some loss of luxury; there will be somewhat more need of labor to procure the necessaries of life. When this is said, all is said. If we have the country, the whole country, the Union, the Constitution, free government—with these will return all the blessings of a well ordered civilization. The path of the country will be a career of greatness and glory, such, as in the olden times, our fathers saw in the dim visions of years yet to come, and such as would have been ours to-day, had it not been for that treason for which the Senator from Kentucky too often seeks to apologize."

10

THE BATTLE OF " BALL'S BLUFF"—COL. BAKER'S DEATH.

On the adjournment of the special session of Congress. Colonel Baker rejoined his regiment in the field, which was attached to, and formed a part of, the Army of Observation on the Potomac. He, however, was restless and uneasy in camp. A vague presentiment of his approaching fate seemed to haunt and oppress him wherever he went. A short time previous to the sanguinary conflict in which he was slain, he is reported as having said to a friend: that, " since his campaign in Mexico. he could never afford to turn his back upon an enemy." and expressed the opinion that he would fall in the first encounter. He returned to Washington, and settled all his affairs. " He went to say farewell to the family of the President. A lady—who in her (then) high position was still gracefully mindful of early friendship—gave him a boquet of late flowers. 'Very beautiful.' he said, quietly, 'These flowers and my memory will wither together.' At night he hastily reviewed his papers. He indicated upon each its proper disposition. 'in case I should not return.' He pressed with quiet earnestness upon his friend, Col. Webb, who deprecated such ghostly instructions, the measures which might become necessary in regard to the resting place of his mortal remains. All this without any ostentation. He performed all these offices, with the coolness of a soldier and a man of affairs, then mounted his horse and rode gayly away to his death."

" On the 20th of October, 1861, the movement of General McCall upon Dranesville having excited the

attention of the enemy at Leesburg, and a regiment of
gray uniforms having been observed cautiously advancing from the west and taking position behind a hill
near Edwards' Ferry, Gen. Stone, comanding the army
of observation on the Potomac, resolved upon armed
reconnoissance to ascertain the position and feel the
strength of the confederate force across the river. A
scouting party sent out from Conrad's Ferry, scoured
the country rapidly in the direction of Leesburg, and
when within about a mile from the town were suddenly
confronted by what, in the uncertain light, appeared to be
rows of tents, but which were afterwards ascertained to be
merely openings in the frontage of the woods. Upon
this report, brought back by the mistaken scouts, Col.
Devens, of the Massachusetts Fifteenth, was ordered to
attack and destroy the supposed camp at daybreak, and
return to Harrison's Island, between Conrad's and
Edwards' Ferries, or, in case he found no enemy, to hold
a secure position and await sufficient force to reconnoiter.
Colonel Baker was ordered to have his Californians at
Conrad's Ferry at sunrise, and the rest of his brigade
to move early.

"Col. Devens crossed the Potomac and proceeded to
the point indicated, and General Stone ordered a party
of Van Allen's cavalry, under Major Mix, accompanied
by that most accomplished of English dragoons, Captain
Stewart, to advance along the Leesburg road, and
ascertain the condition of the heights in the vicinity of
the enemy's battery near Goose Creek. This was performed in dashing style. They came upon a Mississippi

regiment, received and returned its fire, and brought off a prisoner.

"Meantime, Colonel Devens had discovered the error in regard to the supposed encampment, and had been attacked by a superior force of the enemy (under command of Gen. Evans) and fallen back in good order upon the position of Colonel Lee, who had been posted to support him on the bluff. Presently he again advanced, his men, as General Stone reported, behaving admirably, fighting, retiring and advancing in order, and exhibiting every proof of high courage and good discipline.

"At this juncture, Colonel Baker, who, early in the morning (of the 21st) had conferred with the commanding general at Edwards' Ferry, and received his orders from him, began transporting his brigade across the the narrow but deep channel that ran between Harrison's Island and the Virginia shore. The means of transportation were lamentably deficient—three small boats and a scow, which the soldiers say was miserably heavy and water-logged. With such means, the crossing was slow and tedious. While they were toiling across, Devens and Lee, with their little commands, were in desperate peril in front; the wide battalions of the enemy closing around them, with savage prudence availing themselves of every advantage of ground, and flanking by the power of numbers the handful of heroes they dared not attack in front. Baker was not the man to deliberate long when the death-knell of his friends was ringing in his ears in the steady, continuous rattle of the rebel musketry. He advanced to the relief of Devens with a battalion of his Californians under Wistar, the most gallant of the fighting Quakers, and a portion of the 20th Massachusetts. With this devoted band, 1720 men all told, for more than an hour he stood the fire of the surrounding and hidden foe, as from the concealing crescent of the trees they poured their murderous volleys. Bramhall and French struggled up the precipitous banks with a field-piece and two howitzers, which did good service till the gunners dropped dead, and the officers hauled them to the rear to prevent their falling into the enemy's hands. Every man there fought in that hopeless struggle as bravely as if victory were among the possibilities. No thought was there of flight or surrender, even when all but honor was lost. Their duty was to stand there till they were ordered away. Death was merely an incident of the performance of that duty ; and the coolest man there was the Colonel commanding. He talked hopefully and cheerily to his men, even while his heart was sinking with the sun, and the grim presence of disaster and ruin was with him. He was ten paces in their front, where all might see him and take pattern by him. He carried his left hand nonchalantly in his breast, and criticised the firing as quietly as if on parade : "Lower, boys! Steady there! Keep cool now, fire low, and the day is ours."*

All at once a sudden sheet of fire burst from the curved covert of the enemy, and Edward Dickinson Baker fell pierced by eight leaden messengers, freighted with death, from the guns of the advancing foe ; and

---

*Sketch of Col. Baker, by John Hay.

his life-blood, as it quickly flowed from the mortal wounds, mingled with that of the thousands of others that had already moistened the soil of the Old Dominion, and made it historic ground forever.

Thus died, heroically, in the ripe maturity of his manhood, and in the meridian of his fame, one, who forms but another mournful example of the truth of the oft-quoted line of the poet Gray—

> "The paths of glory lead but to the grave."

As a part of the history of this battle, and of Baker's connection with the same, we insert the following copies of the orders (published at the time) from Gen. Stone to Colonel Baker, which were found in the lining of the latter's hat by Captain Young, his aid, after the body had been taken from the field. Both orders were stained with Baker's blood; and one of the bullets, which went through his head, carried away a corner of the first:

"HEADQUARTERS, EDWARDS' FERRY,}
Oct. 21st, 1861. }

" COL. E. D. BAKER:

" *Colonel*—In case of heavy firing in front of Harrison's Island, you will advance the California regiment of your brigade, or retire the regiments under Colonels Lee and Devens, now on the Virginia side of the river, at your discretion—assuming command on arrival.

Very respectfully and truly, your obd't serv't,

"CHAS. P. STONE, Commanding Brigade."

The second order was delivered on the battle field by Col. Cogswell, who, in reply to a question what it meant, said " all right, go ahead." Whereupon Colonel Baker, it is said, put the order in his hat without reading it. An hour afterwards he fell:

" HEADQUARTERS, CORPS OF OBSERVATION,
EDWARDS' FERRY, Oct. 21st, 11:50.

" E. D. BAKER, Commanding Brigade :

" *Colonel*—I am informed that the force of the enemy is about 4,000, all told. If you can push them you may do so, as far as to have a strong position near Leesburg if you can keep them before you, avoiding their batteries. If they pass Leesburg and take the Gum Springs road, you will not follow far, but seize the first good position and cover the road. Their design is to draw us on, if they are obliged to retreat, as far as Goose Creek, where they can be re-inforced from Manassas, and have a strong position. Report frequently, so that when they are pushed, Gorman can come upon their flank.

" Yours respectfully,

" CHAS. P. STONE, Brig. Gen. Commanding."*

HIS FUNERAL OBSEQUIES.

Immediately upon the death of Colonel Baker, his body was carried back from the battle field by his faithful comrades-in-arms, to the Maryland shore. It was subsequently embalmed and removed to Washington City. Appropriate funeral honors were there paid to his remains, after which they were transported to New

---

*It may not be improper here to remark, that General Stone was very severely censured by many of the public journals and public men of the day, on account of the disaster that befell the Federal arms at the battle of Ball's Bluff. Without waiting in the least for an investigation of the matter—nor is this strange, considering the violence of men's passions and the perversity of their judgments, in those exciting times—they threw the entire responsiblity of the movement upon him. His subsequent removal from his command, his long and rigorous confinement, and final release without a trial, are a part of the history of the late war. In all this, great injustice was doubtless done to a gallant and patriotic officer—who, as we are informed, has always claimed that, in directing the advance across the Potomac on that occasion, he was simply acting in obedience to orders from the authorities at Washington ; and hence was not to be held responsible for the fatal results attending that advance.

City, and thence by steamer, at the public charge, to
California. Safely were they borne through the portals
of the Golden Gate at San Francisco ; sadly and affec-
tionately were they received by her citizens, and
peacefully do they now lie entombed on an elevated site,
in Lone Mountain Cemetery of that city, overlooking the
placid waters of her magnificent bay.

> " Slowly and sadly we laid him down,
> From the field of his fame fresh and gory ;
> We carved not a line, we raised not a stone,
> But left him alone in his glory."

The tidings of Colonel Baker's death fell heavily upon
the ears of the American people, accustomed though
they were to the recital of tales of blood. He
had won a reputation co-extensive with the Union by
his eloquence in council, and his heroism in the field,
and was linked to the hearts of the masses by many
endearing ties, which they were loth to sever. Among
the numerous public testimonials to the merits of the
deceased, appearing at the time, is the following general
order issued by Major General McClellan, then in command of the Army of the Potomac :

" HEADQUARTERS, ARMY POTOMAC,}
WASHINGTON, Oct. 22d, 1861. }

(General Order No. 32.)

" The Major General Commanding, with sincere sorrow, announces
the death of Colonel Edward D. Baker, who fell gloriously in battle on
on the afternoon of Monday the 21st of October, [1861,] near Leesburg,
Virginia. The gallant dead had many titles to honor. At the time
of his death, he was a member of the United States Senate from
Oregon ; and it is no injustice to any survivor to say, that one of the
most eloquent voices in that illustrious body has been silenced by his
fall.

"As a patriot, zealous for the honor and interests of his adopted country, he has been distinguished in two wars, and has now sealed with his blood his devotedness to the National flag. Cut off in the fullness of his powers as a statesman, and in the course of a brilliant career as a soldier, while the country mourns his loss, his brothers in arms will envy, while they lament, his fate. He died as a soldier would wish to die, amid the shock of battle, by voice and example, animating his men to brave deeds.

" The remains of the deceased will be interred in this city, with the honors due his rank, and the funeral arrangements will be ordered by Brig. Gen. Silas Casey. As an appropriate mark of respect to the memory of the deceased, the usual badge of mourning will be worn, for the period of thirty days, by the officers of the brigade lately under his command.

" By command of Major Gen. McClellan,
" L. Williams, Ass't Adj't. General."

Upon the assembling of Congress in December, 1861, the death of Senator Baker was appropriately announced in the Senate by his colleague, Mr. Nesmith. The customary resolutions were passed by both Houses, and speeches made eulogizing the life and public services of the deceased. From among the many brilliant, scholarly, and finished tributes to his memory on that occasion, we have selected the remarks of the Hon. O. H. Browning, of Illinois; of the late Hon. James A. McDougall, of California, and of the Hon. Schuyler Colfax, of Indiana, which will be found in a subsequent part of this work.

GENERAL VIEWS OF HIS CHARACTER.

In the preceding pages, we have traced, somewhat concisely, and imperfectly it may be, the career of Edward D. Baker from his cradle in the Old World, through a singularly eventful history of half a century, to his grave in the New. But before leaving our eminent subject, let us take a general survey of his character, and see what manner of man he was.

In looking at his rather complex organization, perhaps the first thing to fix the attention of the critical observer is his individuality—his disposition not to follow in the beaten track of every day existence, but to strike out for himself a new, and hitherto unexplored path in the wilderness of human life.

Few men have had so checkered a career; and fewer still have been so successful in all that they have undertaken. He had that degree of self-confidence and self-reliance which prompted him to dare and do almost anything, within the limit of human exertion. This peculiarity he early manifested in matters which were of but trival importance within themselves. For example: When the captain of a military company in Springfield, he was known, on muster days, to take the drum out of the hands of the regular drummer and try his own hand to show his young companions what an admirable drummer he was, or might be. Again, during his connection with the Christian church, he used to take the lead in singing, and believed that he could sing a little better, perhaps, than any one else.

After making a speech, it was his habit—no very uncommon thing, however, among public speakers—to inquire of his friends what they thought of it? and, not unfrequently, he would depreciate his best efforts for the purpose of eliciting their commendation. He was careless of his attire, yet proud of his personal presence. Nothing, it is said, pleased him more than to be told that he resembled the first Napoleon; and there was some resemblance between them.

In common with the majority of aspiring men, Colonel Baker loved praise, and courted popular favor; but, unlike that majority, he had the ability to command both. He was born, as it were, with a keen thirst for glory, and persistently sought the bubble, reputation, even at the cannon's mouth. This was doubtless the main cause of that restless activity which marked his life. Hence, he was never fully satisfied with any position attained in any of the varied walks in which he trod; but was all the while struggling to bring himself up to some ideal level, above and beyond the range of common effort and success.

As an illustration of his vaulting ambition, we are told, that, in early manhood, while yet a resident of Carrollton, Illinois, he was once found by an acquaintance in a retired locality, weeping, and looking as disconsolate as the exiled Marius sitting upon the ruins of ancient Carthage. On being interrogated as to the cause of his unusual grief, he replied: "Oh! I was just thinking how unlucky I am to have been born in old England, for now, I can never be President."*

Colonel Baker has been very properly called a "many sided man," presenting many different phases of character, and all of these more or less calculated to attract and please. "His very weaknesses became instruments of fascination. His egotism, his vanity and personal frailties, were all genial, and gave him an irresistible claim to sympathy." Without any of those adventitious advantages of family, fortune, connections or patronage; self prompted, self-sustained, and self-taught, [saving the early instruction given him by his father in the rudiments of knowledge] he surmounted every obstacle, carved his way to eminence, became one of the ornaments of the nation, and "died a Senator in Congress." For all this, he is deserving of high praise. But it is undeniable that his many splendid virtues were alloyed with something of that dross which debases our common humanity, and from which the noblest natures are not wholly exempt. It is not our purpose, now and here, to unveil his faults—which at the worst were but of the negative kind—and hold them up to the public gaze, though the great English bard has said,

> " The evil that men do lives after them,
> The good is oft interred with their bones."

So, let it not be with our Baker.

As a brilliant, fascinating, and effective forensic speaker, he must ever be held in high regard. He had

---

*This story has long been current among Baker's old friends and boon companions; and whether true or false, shows to some extent the character of the man.

been led, in his youth, to embrace the profession of law, because the very nature of the calling afforded his mind excitement, and kept his faculties in active, unceasing play. He, moreover, very naturally, and, as society is constituted in this country, properly viewed it as the main avenue to social advancement, to political influence and reputation, and the stepping stone to the highest honors attainable in a free State. When a boy, he had read the history of the great lights of the profession, both of England and America—many of whom rose from the humblest walks of life to wealth, to station, to power—and his aspiring soul burned with an unquenchable ardor to emulate their examples, and win for himself a name which might live on the page of history, and in the memories of men, long after the earthly house of his tabernacle had dissolved and mingled with its mother dust.

Possessed of the requisite natural qualifications, had he confined his attention solely to the law, and applied himself with like assiduity and perseverance, he might have become the Erskine of the American bar. But it was in other fields, rather, than the forum, that he sought to realize his highest ambition.

Colonel Baker, as before noticed, commenced his political life as a Whig of the Henry Clay and Daniel Webster school, and acted with that party until its final dismemberment after the Presidential canvass of 1852, when he united his fortunes with the newly formed Republican party. His course as a politician was marked by much courtesy and liberality of sentiment towards his opponents; by more than ordinary boldness and independence of spirit, and oft-times by the most enlarged and statesman-like views. Yet, upon the whole, he seemed to have lacked, in some degree, that solidity of character—that steadiness, and unyielding adherence to fixed principles and definite lines of public policy, which are essential to the great and successful political leader.

But whatever contrariety of opinion may exist with reference to Baker's political character and influence, it will hardly be denied that he was an orator of the highest order. More eminent he may have been for the lighter graces than the severer qualities of oratory, yet not incapable of close, connected, logical reasoning. His success was no doubt partially owing to those superior personal attractions which he had received from the hand of nature; for an audience likes to look upon him who addresses them, reading grace and dignity in his physical form, whilst catching inspiration from his lips. His range and versatility as a speaker were such that he could command, at will, the "applause of listening Senates," and, anon, the hearty plaudits of of an unlettered frontier audience. He was especially great on great occasions, generally rising above, instead of falling below the expectations of his hearers.

"His voice," says Senator Sumner, "was not full or sonorous, but sharp and clear. It was penetrating rather than commanding; and yet when touched by his ardent nature, it became sympathetic, and even musical. His countenance, body and gesture, all showed the unconscious inspiration of his voice, and he went on—master of his audience, master also of himself. All his faculties were completely at his command. Ideas, illustrations, words, seemed to come unbidden, and to range themselves in harmonious forms, as, in the walls of ancient Thebes, each stone took its proper place of its own accord, moved only by the music of a lyre. His fame as a speaker was so peculiar, even before he appeared among us, that it was sometimes supposed he might lack those solid powers without which the oratorical faculty itself can exercise only a transient influence. But his speeches on this floor * * * showed that his matter was as good as his manner, and that while he was master of fence, he was also master of ordnance. His controversy was graceful, sharp, and flashing like a cimeter, but his argument was powerful and sweeping like a battery."*

His style was nervous, elegant and copious. Many of the finest passages in his speeches were put in the form of interrogatories, gaining thereby immeasurably in force and effect. His mind teemed with beautiful images, comparisons, poetical quotations, and classical allusions, which were scattered with profusion, and glittered like pearls among all his efforts. His command of the English language, however, "was so full and complete as to tempt him sometimes to indulge in an affluence of diction, too ornate and copious to satisfy the strictest canons of criticism." What has been said concerning the style of the Irish orator, Henry Grattan,

---

* Vide Mr. Sumner's remarks on the death of Baker, in the Congressional Globe for the session of 1861-2, page 54.

by one of his biographers, may, with almost equal
propriety, be applied to Baker's:

"There was nothing common-place in his thoughts, his
images, or his sentiments. Everthing came fresh from
his mind with the vividness of a new creation. His most
striking chareteristic was condensation and rapidity of
thought. His forte was reasoning, but it was 'logic on
fire;' and he seemed ever to delight in flashing his ideas
on the mind with a sudden, startling abruptness."

The examples already supplied, will aid the reader in
forming some idea, however inadequate, of his marvelous
eloquence; but much of its force and effect was necessarily lost with the delivery. The orator himself must
have been seen and heard in order to be truly appreciated.

"It requires but a very slight acquaintance with the
laws and aptitudes of mind," says the late Bishop
Bascom—himself one of the most eloquent of men—" to
know that on the score of warmth, interest and impression, the speaker has greatly the advantage over the
writer, and the hearer over the reader. The personal,
in speaking and hearing, is found to be very different
from the ideal in reading and writing. With the speaker
and hearer, the eye, hand, action, intent gaze, and
intuitive sympathy, all have an emphasis unknown to
the mere writer and reader. Between the latter the
distance is greater. * * * The unstudied inspiration
of the speaker at the moment, even when the language
is the same—the intensified thought and feeling of
public address, are of necessity lost when the discourse
is but simply read."

Mrs. Welby, the poetess, has given expression to the same thought in these exquisitely beautiful lines:

> "There's a charm in delivery, a magical art,
> That thrills like a kiss from the lips to the heart;
> Tis the glance—the expression—the well chosen word—
> By whose magic the depths of the spirit are stirred;
> The smile—the mute gesture—the soul-stirring pause—
> The eyes sweet expression, that melts while it awes—
> The lips soft persuasion—its musical tone:
> Oh! such were the charms of that eloquent one."

It is to be regretted that many of Baker's happiest effusions and richest gems of thought were never transferred to paper. They passed away with the occasions that called them forth, or live only in the memories of those who heard them. To illustrate: In the earlier portion of his public life, he delivered an erudite and eloquent discourse on Art, before a literary society in Jacksonville, Illinois, which was greatly admired. At another time he delivered a brilliant and finished lecture in Springfield. Subsequently, in 1858, he made a magnificent speech at a celebration in San Francisco, on the occasion of laying the first Atlantic cable, which was replete with passages of the highest sublimity and beauty. To these may be added his multitudinous forensic and political harangues, some of which were regarded, at the time, as productions of the rarest merit. But he led too busy and nomadic a life to bestow much attention upon these scattered offspring of his brain, after they had served a present purpose. And, now, that the voiceless grave has closed over him, they, too, are being entombed beneath the rapidly accumulating rubbish of years.

12

It used to be a saying with the members of a certain political party in this country, that "they were always in favor of the next war." Colonel Baker might well have been classed in that list; for whenever the nation became involved in war, foreign or domestic, he could not well keep out of it if he would, and he would not if he could. He loved war. Its pomp, its pageantry, and its glory, were all irresistibly attractive to him. Nor was he unwilling to share in its hardships, its sufferings, its sacrifices. Brave, gallant, impetuous, he unquestionably was; yet it is questionable if his courage was always tempered with that coolness, that sagacity and discretion in movement, which characterize the great military chieftain.

He was a thorough cosmopolitan. In the pursuit of the varied objects of his ambition, he was deterred by no differences of country or climate, but trod with equal firmness the Torrid as well as the Temperate zone. Had he lived in the age of the Crusades, he would doubtless have assumed the cross, and led the van in one of those wild and extravagant expeditions to wrest the Holy Land from the dominion of the Moslems. Or, had he flourished in the days of chivalry, he would probably have turned knight-errant; put on a helmet and coat of mail; seized a lance and buckler, mounted some flaming steed, and sallied forth in quest of adventures and glory.

Although not a "native to the manor born," he came to America in his early childhood, and was thoroughly naturalized. Our Constitution and laws, our unity, our honor, our glory, were all alike dear to him. For these he contended on the stump, and in the halls of Congress, with a vehemence, a power and eloquence, at times, almost superhuman. For these he drew his sword in three wars, and for these " alas! he died."

In addition to his many other endowments, Colonel Baker was also a poet of no mean pretensions, as will appear from the following lines addressed to the Ocean wave, and given on the authority of one of his Congressional eulogists :

"It were vain to ask as thou rollest afar,
Of banner or mariner, of ship or star ;
It were vain to seek in thy stormy face,
Some tale of the sorrowful past to trace.
Thou art swelling high, thou art flashing free ;
How vain are the questions we ask of thee.

"I, too, am a wave on a stormy sea;
I, too, am a wanderer driven like thee ;
I, too, am seeking a distant land,
To be lost and gone ere I reach the strand ;
For the land I seek is a waveless shore,
And they who once reach it shall wander no more."

With very few of our public men can Edward Dickinson Baker be compared ; for he was an original genius—a man of his own kind. There is one, however, to whom he bore a very considerable resemblance. We refer to the late Honorable S. S. Prentiss, of Mississippi. Like Prentiss, Baker was the child of poverty, and trained in the rugged school of adversity. Like him, he was the builder of his own fortune—adopted the profession of law, and rose to distinction by virtue of his

superior gifts as an advocate. Like him, his speeches were
"argumentative without formality, brilliant without
gaudiness." Like him, he possessed a refined and
scholarly taste, a poetic and imaginative soul, which
readily appreciated, and could give expression to, all
that was beautiful in language, glowing in sentiment,
rich in illustration, and grand in imagery. Like him,
on important occasions, when called upon to speak, he
came glowing up to his theme, and

> "Where fancy weary grew in other men,
>   His fresh as morning rose."

Like him, he ardently thirsted for political honors,
which when he had won he but lightly esteemed.
Like him, he possessed a warm, enthusiastic and genial
temperament, which sought the companionship of
kindred spirits, and entered with zest into all the pleas-
ures and amusements of social life. Like Prentiss, he
was generous to a fault; yet, in the exuberance of that
generosity, he, perhaps, sometimes forgot to be just.

" Every trait of his noble nature was in excess. His
very virtues leaned to faults ; and his faults themselves
to virtues. The like of him I ne'er shall see again, so
compounded was he of all sorts of contradictions, without a single element in him to disgust—without one
characteristic which did not attract and charm. His
public exhibitions were all splendid and glorious. He
did anything he attempted magnificently, well ; and yet
as I knew him, he could hardly be called a man of
business. He was a natural spendthrift, and yet despised
debt and dependence. He was heedless of all conse-

quences, yet of the soundest judgment in council and discretion in movement. He was almost the only man I ever saw, whom I never heard utter a scandal ; and he had the least charity of any man I ever saw, for all kinds of baseness or meanness. He was continually, without ceasing, quoting classic lore, and not the least of a pedant. He was brave to fool-hardiness, and would not hurt Uncle Toby's fly."*

But Baker, the genial companion, the shining advocate, the accomplished orator and chivalrous soldier, has gone from among the living ! gone forever to the shadowy realms of the spirit land !

> "The sun that illumin'd that planet of clay
> Had sunk in the west of an unclouded day,
> And the cold dews of death stood like diamonds of light,
> Thickly set in the pale dusky forehead of night ;
> From each gleamed a ray of that fetterless soul
> Which had bursted its prison, despising control,
> And careering above, o'er earth's darkness and gloom,
> Inscribed ' I still live' on the arch of the tomb."

Illinois, during the half century of her existence as a State, has produced many eminent men. She can already boast a long catalogue of " dead heroes and statesmen," who severally won imperishable honor at the forum, on the hustings, in the Legislative halls, or by deeds of deathless daring on historic battle fields. The names of an Edwards, a Reynolds, a Henry, a Hardin, a Ford, a Harris, a Bissell, a Douglas, a Lincoln, a McDougall, and last, though not least, a Baker, will live as long as

---

*Memoir of S. S. Prentiss, by Henry A. Wise.

the lettered page of the State's history, and swell the tide of her glory.

Be it then the province of the living, who would achieve like renown, to emulate their bright examples, to imitate their noble deeds, and cherish their great names to an everlasting memory.

APPENDIX.

Mr. President :—On taking my seat in the Senate at its special session, in July last, my first active participation in its business was on the occasion of the proceedings commemorative of the death of the Hon. Stephen A. Douglas, my immediate predecessor ; and now, sir, at the commencement of this, my second session, it becomes my melancholy duty to bear a part in the ceremonies in honor of another who had been longer a citizen of the State of Illinois, whose memory is not less dear to the hearts of her people, and whose tragical and untimely death has shrouded the State in mourning.

Hon. Edward D. Baker was, and had ever been, my personal and political friend, and, from earliest manhood, the relations between us had been of the closest and most confidential character that friendship allows ; and there are but few whose death would have left so large a void in my affections.

Something my junior in years, he was my senior in the profession to which we both belonged, and commencing our professional career in the same State, and very near the same time, traveling much upon the same circuit, and belonging to the same political party, a friendship grew up which was cemented and strengthened by time, and continued from our first acquaintance amid the collisions of the bar, and the rivalries of politics, without ever having sustained a shock or an interruption. even for a moment ; and I owe it to the memories of the past, and to the relations which subsisted between us whilst he lived, to offer some poor tribute to his worth, now that he is dead.

Few men who have risen to positions of great distinction and usefulness, and left the impress of their lives upon their country's history, have been less indebted to the circumstances of birth and fortune. He inherited neither ancestral wealth nor honors; but whatever of either he attained, was the reward of his own energy and talents. He was, very literally, the "architect of his own fortune." Commencing the practice of law before he had reached the full maturity of manhood, and in what was then a border State, but among lawyers whose talents and learning shed luster upon the profession to which they belonged, without the patronage of wealth or power, he soon made his way to the front rank of the bar, and maintained his position there to the hour of his death.

But he did not confine himself exclusively to professional pursuits, and to the care of his own private affairs. He was a man of rare endowments, and of such fitness and aptitude for public employments as were sure to attract public attention. He could not, if he would, have made his way through life along its quiet, peaceful, and secluded walks; and it does him no discredit to say, that he would not if he could.

He was too fully in sympathy with his kind to be indifferent to anything which affected their welfare, and too heroic in character to remain a passive spectator of great and stirring events. He was eminently a man of action; and although fond of literature and science and art, and possessed of a refined and cultivated taste, he yet loved the sterner conflicts of life more than the quiet conquests of the closet; and whilst a citizen of Illinois, served her both as soldier and civilian, and won distinction wherever he acted. He had elasticity, strength, versatility and fervor of intellect, and a mind full of resources.

His talents were both varied and brilliant, and capable of great achievements; but their usefulness was, perhaps, somewhat impaired by a peculiarity of physical organization which made him one of the most restless of men, and incapable of the close, steady and persevering mental application, without which great results cannot often be attained. It was not fickleness or unsteadiness of purpose, but a proud and impatient spurning of restraint, contempt for the beaten track of mental process, and disgust with the dullness and weariness of confinement and inaction. But this defect was, to a very great extent, compensated by the wonderful ease and rapidity with which he would master any subject upon which he chose to concentrate the powers of his mind—by the marvelous facility with which he acquired knowledge, and the felicity with which he could use it.

Whatever he could do at all, he could do at once, and up to the full measure of his capacity. Whatever he could comprehend at all, he comprehended with the quickness of intuition, and gained but little afterwards by investigation and elaboration. He did not reach intellectual results as other men do, by the slow processes of analysis or induction, but if he could reach them at all, he could do it at a bound. And yet it was not jumping at conclusions, for he could always state with almost mathematical clearness and precision the premises from which he made his deductions, and guide you along the same path he had traveled to the same goal. He saw at a glance all the material, and all the relations of the material, which he intended to use, to the subject in hand, but which another would have carefully and laboriously to search out and collect to be enabled to see at all, and diligently to collate before understanding its uses and relations.

To a greater extent than most men, he combined the force and severity of logic with grace, fancy and eloquence, filling at the bar at the same time the character of the astute and profound lawyer, and the able, eloquent and successful advocate; whilst in the Senate, the wise, prudent and discreet statesman was combined with the chaste, classical, brilliant and persuasive orator.

But with all his aptitude for, and adaptation to, the highest and noblest pursuits of the civilian, he had a natural taste, talent and fondness for the life of the soldier. There was something in the bugle-blast of war, and the cannon's roar, which roused his soul to its profoundest depths, and he could no more remain in inglorious ease at home, while the desolations of war blackened and blasted the land, than the proud eagle could descend from his home in the clouds to dwell with the moping owl.

Three times, in his not protracted life, he led our citizen soldiers to the embattled plain to meet in deadly conflict his country's foes. Alas !

13

that he shall lead them no more; that he shall never more marshal them for the glorious strife—never more rouse to the "signal trumpet tone." He has fallen! "The fresh dust is chill upon the breast that burned erewhile with fires that seemed immortal."

> "He sleeps his last sleep—he has fought his last battle;
> No sound shall awake him to glory again."

He fell—as I think he would have preferred to fall, had he the choice of the mode of death—in the storm of battle, cheering his brave followers on to duty in the service of his adopted country, to which he felt that he owed much; which he loved well, and had served long and faithfully. It does him no dishonor to say that he was a man of great ambition, and that he yearned after military renown; but his ambition was chastened by his patriotism, his strong sense of justice, and his humanity; and its fires never burned so fiercely in his bosom as to tempt him to purchase honor, glory, and distinction for himself by needlessly sacrificing, or even imperiling, the lives of others. He was no untried soldier, with a name yet to win. It was already high on the roll of fame, and indissolubly linked with his country's history. Years ago, at home and abroad, he had drawn his sword in his country's cause, and shed his blood in defense of her rights. Years ago, he had led our soldiers to battle, and by his gallantry shed new lustre on our arms, and historic interest upon Cerro Gordo's heights; and now he had that fame to guard and protect. He had to defend his already written page of history from blot or stain, as well as to add to it another leaf equally radiant and enduring. But, Mr. President, it would be a poor, inadequate, and unworthy estimate of his character which should explore only a selfish ambition, and aspirations for individual glory for the sources of his action.

The impelling causes were far higher and nobler. He was a true, immovable, incorruptible and unshrinking patriot. He was the fast, firm friend of civil and religious liberty, and believed that they should be the common heritage and blessing of all mankind, and that they could be secured and enjoyed only through the instrumentality of organized constitutional government, and submission to and obedience of its laws; and the conviction on his mind was deep and profound that if the wicked rebellion, which had been inaugurated, went unrebuked, and treason triumphed over law, Constitutional government in North America would be utterly annihilated, to be followed by the confusion of anarchy, and the confusions of anarchy to be succeeded by the oppressions and atrocities of despotism. He believed that whatever the horrors and plagues and desolation of civil war might be, they would still be far less in magnitude and duration than the plagues and calamities which would inevitably follow upon submission and separation. The contest in which we are engaged had been, without cause, or pretext of cause, forced upon us. We had to accept the strife, or so submit to an arrogant assumption of superiority of right as to show ourselves unworthy of the liberties and blessings, which the blood and treasure and wisdom and virtue of illustrious sires had achieved for us; and he believed that the issue of the contest was powerfully and virtually to affect the welfare and happiness of the American people, if not indeed of all other nations, for centuries yet to be. With these views, both just and patriotic, he recognized it as his duty to give his services to his country whenever, and in whatever capacity, they could be of most value and importance; and with as much of self-abnegation as the frailties of humanity would allow, he took his place in the serried ranks of war, and in the strict and discreet discharge of his duty as a soldier, fighting for his country in a holy cause, he fell.

And it is, Mr. President, to me, his friend, a source of peculiar gratification that the history of the disastrous day which terminated his brilliant career, when it shall have been truthfully written, will be his full and sufficient vindication from any charge of temerity or recklessness regarding the lives of those intrusted to his care. He was brave, ardent and impetuous, and "when war's stern strength was on his soul," he no doubt felt that "one crowded hour of glorious life was worth an age without a name." But his was not the fitful impetuosity of the whirlwind, which unfits for self-control or the command of others, but the strong, steady, and resistless roll of the stream within its prescribed limits, and to its sure and certain object; not the impetuosity which culminates in fantastic rashness, but that which in the presence of danger is exalted to the sublimity of heroism.

I have said that he was ambitious, but there was never ambition
with less of the taint and dross of selfishness. He was incapable of
a mean and unmanly envy, and was ever quick to perceive and ready
to acknowledge the merit of a rival, and would stifle his own desires
and postpone his own aggrandizement for the advancement of a friend.
Nobly generous, he could and did make sacrifices of both pecuniary
and political advantages to his friendships, which, with him, were real,
sincere and lasting. He never sought to drag others down from moral
or social, professional or political eminence, that he might rise upon
the ruin, nor regarded the good fortune of another, in whatever vocation or department in life, as a wrong done him, or as any impediment
to his own prosperity. Brave and self-reliant, but neither rash nor
presumptuous, he could avenge or forgive an injury with a grace and
promptitude which did equal honor to his boldness of spirit and kindness of heart. Under insult or indignity, he was fierce and defiant,
and could teach an enemy alike to fear and respect him, and, in the
collisions of life's battle, may have given something of the impression
of harshness of temper; but in the domestic circle, amid the social
throng, and under friendship's genial and enchanting influences, he
was as gentle and confiding in his affections as a woman, and as tender
and trustful as a child.

Senator Baker was not only a lawyer, an orator, a statesman, and a
soldier, but he was also a poet, and at all times, when deeply in earnest,
both spoke and acted under high poetic inspiration. At one time,
when I traveled upon the same circuit with him, and others who have
since been renowned in the history of Illinois, it was no uncommon
thing, after the labors of the day in court were ended, and forensic
battles had been lost and won, for the lawyers to forget the asperities
which had been engendered by the conflicts of the bar in the innocent,
if not profitable, pastime of writing verses for the amusement of each
other and their friends; and I well remember with what greater facility
than others, he could dash from his pen effusions sparkling all over
with poetic gems; and if all that he has thus written could be collected
together, it would make no mean addition to the poetic literature of
our country. Its beauty, grace and vivacity, would certainly redeem
it from oblivion.

Yet he did not aspire to the character of a poet, but wrought the poetic vein only for the present amusement of himself and intimate friends, and I am not aware that any of the productions of which I speak ever passed beyond that limited circle. They were not perpetuated by " the art preservative of all arts."

The same thing is true of his forensic efforts, many of which were distinguished by a brilliancy, power and eloquence, and a classic grace and purity that would have done honor to the most renowned barrister, which live now only in the traditions of the country. Stenography, was, at that day, an unknown art in Illinois, and writing out a speech would have been a prodigality of time and labor of which an Illinois lawyer was probably never guilty.

To Senators who were his cotemporaries here, and who have heard the melody of his voice, who have witnessed his powerful and impassioned bursts of eloquence, and felt the witchery of the spell that he has thrown upon them, it were vain for me to speak of his displays in this Chamber. It is no disparagement to his survivors to say, that he stood the peer of any gentlemen on this floor in all that constitutes the able and skillful debater, and the classical, persuasive and enchanting orator.

But his clear and manly voice shall be heard in these halls no more. Never again shall these crowded galleries hang breathless on his words ; never again the thronging multitudes who gathered where'er he spoke be thrilled by the magic of his eloquence. The voice that could soothe to delicious repose, or rouse to a tempest of passion, is now hushed forever. The heart once so fiery, brave, lies pulseless in the tomb, and all that is left to his country or his home is the memory of of what he was.

I will not attempt, Mr. President, to speak poor, cold words of sympathy and consolation to the stricken hearts of his family. I know, sir, how bitter and immedicable their anguish is. I know, sir, how it rends the heart-strings, all willing though we be, to lay our loved ones as sacrifices even on our country's altar. The death-dealing hand of war has invaded my own household and slain its victim there, and I know that words bring no healing to the grief which follows these bereavements. The heart turns despairingly away from the " honor's 'voice," which provokes not the silent dust, and from the flatteries which cannot

> " Soothe the dull cold ear of death ;"

And the spirits ebb, and

> " Life's enchanting scenes their lustre lose,
>   And lessen in our sight."

Time alone can bring healing on its wing—

> "Time ! the beautifier of the dead,
>   Adorner of the ruin, comforter
>   And only healer when the heart hath bled,"

Can only mitigate, chasten, and sanctify the crushing sorrow. And not till after time has done its gentle work, and stilled the tempest of feeling, can the sorrowing hearts around his now desolate hearthstone find consolation in remembering how worthily he lived, and how gloriously he died—that he is "fortune's now, and fame's ;" and that when peace, on downy pinions, comes again to bless our troubled land, and all hearts have renewed their allegiance to the beneficent Government for which he died, history will claim him as its own, and canonize him in the hearts of his countrymen as a heroic martyr in the great cause of human rights, and chronicle his deeds on pages illuminated with the gratitude of freemen, and as imperishable as the love of liberty.

REMARKS OF THE LATE HON. JAMES A. M'DOUGALL, IN THE SENATE.

Mr. President :—Within the brief period I have occupied a seat on this floor, I have listened to the announcement of the decease of the two Senators nearest to me by the ties of association and friendship, both representative men, and among the ablest that ever discoursed counsel in this Senate.

I trust I shall be pardoned if it be thought there is something of pride in my claim of friendship with such distinguished and not to be forgotten men.

The late Senator from Illinois, as well as the late Senator of whom I am about to speak, were my seniors in years, and much more largely instructed than myself in public affairs. Differing as they had for a period of more than a quarter of a century, they had met together, and in the maintenance in all its integrity of the great governmental institution of our fathers, they were one. Coming myself a stranger to your counsels, I looked to them for that home advice in which there is no purpose of disguise or concealment.

Their loss has been, and is, to me, like the shadows of great clouds; but while I have felt, and now feel, their loss, as companions, friends and counselors, in whose truth I trusted, I feel that no sense of private loss should find expression when a nation suffers. I may say here, however, that, while for the loss of these two great Senators a nation suffers, the far country from whence I come, feels the sufferings of a double loss. They were both soldiers and champions of the West—of our new and undeveloped possessions. A few months since, the people of the Pacific, from the sea of Cortez to the straits of Fuca, mourned for *Douglas*; the same people now mourn for *Baker*. The two Senators were widely different men, molded in widely different forms, and they walked in widely different paths; but the tread of their hearts kept time, and they each sought a common goal, only by different paths.

The record of the honorable birth, brilliant life, and heroic death of the late Edward Dickinson Baker has been already made by a thousand eloquent pens. That record has been read in cabin and in hall, from Maine to farthest Oregon. I offer now but to pay to his memory the tribute of my love and praise. While paying this tribute with a proud sadness, I trust its value will not be diminished when I state, that, for many years, and until the recent demands of patriotism extinguished controversial differences, we were almost constant adversaries in the forum and at the bar.

A great writer, in undertaking to describe one of the greatest men, said: "Know that there is not one of you who is aware of his real nature." I think that, with all due respect, I might say of the late Senator the same thing to this Senate, as I was compelled to say it to myself. Of all the men I have ever known, he was the most difficult to comprehend.

He was a many-sided man. Will, mind, power, radiated from one center within him in all directions; and while the making of that circle, which, according to the dreams of old philosophy, would constitute a perfect being, is not within human hope he may be regarded as one who at least illustrated the thought.

His great powers cannot be attributed to the work of laborious years. They were not his achievements. They were gifts, God-given. His sensations, memory, thought and action, went hand in hand together with a velocity and power, which, if not always exciting admiration, compelled astonishment.

Although learned, the late Senator was not what is called a scholar. He was too full of stirring life, to labor among the moldy records of dead ages; and had he not been, the wilderness of the West furnished no field for the exercise of mere scholarly acomplishments.

I say the late Senator was learned. He was skilled in metaphysics, logic and law. He might be called a master of history, and of all the literature of our own language. He knew much of music—not only music as it gives present pleasure to the ear, but music in the sense in which it was understood by the old seekers after wisdom, who held that in harmonious sounds rested some of the great secrets of the infinite.

Poetry he inhaled and expressed. The afilatus called *divine* breathed about him. Many years since, on the then wild plains of the West, in the middle of a star-lit night, as we journeyed together, I heard first from him the chant of that noble song, "The Battle of Ivry." Two of its stanzas impressed me then, and there are other reasons why they impress me now:

> "The King has come to marshal us, in all his armor drest,
> And he has bound a snow-white plume upon his gallant crest;
> He looked upon his people, and a tear was in his eye;
> He looked upon the traitors, and his glance was stern and high,
> Right graciously he smiled on us, as ran from wing to wing,
> Down all our line a deafening shout, 'God save our Lord the King!'
> And if my standard-bearer fall, and fall full well he may,
> For never saw I promise yet of such a bloody fray,

Press where ye see my white plume shines, amidst the ranks of war,
And be your oriflamme to-day, the helmet of Navarre.

"Hurrah! the foes are moving; hark the mingled din
Of fife, and steed, and trump, and drum, and roaring culverin;
The fiery Duke is pricking fast across Saint Andre's plain,
With all the hireling chivalry of Gueldre's and Almagne:
Now by the lips of those ye love, fair gentlemen of France,
Charge! for the golden lilies; now upon them with the lance!
A thousand spurs are striking deep, a thousand spears in rest,
A thousand knights are pressing close behind the snow-white crest;
And in they burst, and on they rushed, while, like a guiding star,
Amidst the thickest carnage blazed the helmet of Navarre."

It was the poetry which embodies the life of great and chivalrous action which moved him most, and he possessed the power to create it.

He was an orator—not an orator trained to the model of the Greek or Roman school, but one far better suited to our age and people. He was a master of dialectics, and possessed a power and skill in words, which would have confounded the rhetoric of Gorgias, and demanded of the great master of dialectics himself, the exact use of all his materials of wordy warfare.

He was deeply versed in all that belongs to the relations and conduct of all forms of societies, from families to States, and the laws which have and do govern them. He was not a man of authorities, simply because he used authorities only as the rounds whereby to ascend to principles. Having learned much, he was a remarkable master of all he knew, whether it was to analyze, generalize, or combine his vast materials.

It was true of him, as it is true of most remarkable minds, that he did not always appear to be all he was. The occasion made the measure of the exhibition of his strength. When the occasion challenged the effort, he could discourse as cunningly as the sage of Ithaca, and as wisely as the king of Pylus.

He was a soldier. He was a leader; "a man of war," fit, like the Tachmonite, "to sit in the seat, chief among the captains." Like all men who possess hero blood, he loved fame, glory, honorable renown.

14

He thirsted for it with an ardent thirst, as did Cicero and Cæsar ; and
what was that nectar in which the gods delighted in high Olympus,
but the wine of praise for great deeds accomplished ? Would that he
might have lived, so that his great sacrifice might have been offered,
and his great soul have gone up from some great victorious field, his
lips bathed with the nectar that he loved.

None ever felt more than he—

> " Since all must life resign,
>   Those sweet delights that decorate the brave,   .
> 'Tis folly to decline,
>   And steal inglorious to the silent grave."

But it was something more than the fierce thirst for glory that
carried the late Senator to the field of sacrifice. No one felt more
than he the majestic dignity of the great cause for which our nation
now makes war. He loved freedom ; if you please, Anglo-Saxon freedom ; for he was of that great old race. He loved this land, this whole
land. He had done much to conquer it from the wilderness ; and by
his own acts he had made it his land.

Hero blood is patriot blood. When he witnessed the storm of
anarchy with which the madness of depraved ambition sought to overwhelm the land of his choice and love, when he heard the battle-call,

> " Lay down the axe, fling by the spade,
>   Leave in its track the toiling plow ;
> The rifle and the bayonet blade,
>   For arms like yours are fitter now .
>
> "And let the hands that ply the pen,
>   Quit the light task, and learn to wield
> The horseman's crooked brand, and rein
>   The charger on the battle-field.
>
> "Our country calls ; away ! away !
>   To where the blood-streams blot the green ;
> Strike to defend the gentlest sway,
>   That time in all its course has seen."

It was in the spirit of the patriot hero that the gallant soldier, the grave senator, the white-haired man of counsel, yet full of youth as full of years, gave answer as does the war horse, to the trumpet's sound.

The wisdom of his conduct has been questioned. Many have thought that he should have remained for counsel in this hall. Mr. President, the propriety of a Senator taking upon himself the duties of a soldier, depends, like many other things, on circumstances; and certainly such conduct has the sanction of the example of great names.

Socrates—who was not of the councils of Athens, simply because he deemed his office as a teacher of wisdom a higher and nobler one—did not think it unworthy of himself to serve as a common soldier in battle; and when Plato seeks best to describe, and most to dignifiy, his great master, he causes Alcibiades, among other things, to say of him:

"I ought not to omit what Socrates was in battle; for in that battle after which the generals decreed to me the prize of courage, Socrates alone, of all men, was the savior of my life, standing by me when I had fallen and was wounded, and preserving both myself and my arms from the hands of the enemy. But to see Socrates, when our army was defeated and scattered in flight at Delius, was a spectacle worthy to behold. On that occasion I was among the cavalry, and he on foot heavily armed. After the total rout of our troops, he and Laches retreated together. I came up by chance; and seeing them, bade them be of good cheer, for that I would not leave them. As I was on horseback, and therefore less occupied by a regard of my own situation, I could better observe than at Potidœa, the beautiful spectacle exhibited by Socrates on this emergency. * * * * He walked and darted his regards around with a majestic composure, looking tranquilly both on his friends and enemies, so that it was evident to every one, even from afar, that whoever should venture to attack him would encounter a desperate resistance. He and his companion thus departed in safety; for those who are scattered in flight are pursued and killed, whilst men hesitate to touch those who exhibit such a countenance as that of Socrates, even in defeat."

This is the picture of a sage painted by a sage; and why may not great wisdom be the strongest element of a great war?

In the days when the States of Greece were free, when Rome was free, when Venice was free, who but their great statesmen, counselors, and senators, led their armies to victorious battle ? In the best days of all the great and free states, civil place and distinction were never held inconsistent with military authority and conduct. So far from it, all history teaches the fact that those who have proved most competent to direct and administer the affairs of government, in times of peace, were not only trusted, but were best trusted with the conduct of armies in the time of war.

In these teachings of history there may be some lessons we have yet to learn ; and that we have such lessons to learn I know was the strong conviction of the late Senator.

It is with no sense of satisfaction that I feel it my duty to say, that I have been led to the opinion that there is much soundness in the opinion he entertained.

It is but a brief time since the late Senator was among us, maintaining our country's cause, with wise counsel, clothed in eloquent words. When, in August last, his duties here as a Senator for the time ceased, he devoted himself exclusively to the duties of a soldier. Occupying a subordinate position, commanded, where he was most fit to command, he received his orders. He saw and knew the nature of the enterprise he was required to undertake ; he saw and knew that he was required to move underneath the shadow of the wings of Azrael. He did not, he would not, question the requirement made of him. His motto on that day was: "A good heart and no hope." He knew, as was known at Balaklava, that some one had blundered ; yet he said, " Forward, my brigade, although some one has blundered."

Was this reckless rashness ? No !

It may be called sacrifice, self-sacrifice ; but I who knew the man who was the late Senator—the calm, self-possessed perfectness of his valor, and who have studied all the details of the field of his last offering with a sad earnestness, say to you, sir, to this Senate, to the country, and particularly to the people of the land of the West, where most and best he is known and loved, that no rash, reckless regardlessness of danger can be attributed to him. It is but just to say of him, that his conduct sprung from a stern, hero, patriot, martyr spirit, that enabled him to dare, unflinchingly, with a smile to the green earth, and a smile to the bright heavens, and a cheer to his brave companions, ascend the altar of sacrifice.

A poet of the middle ages, speaking of Carthage as then a dead city, the grave of which was scarcely discernible, says :

" For cities die, kingdoms die ; a little sand and grass cover all that was once lofty in them, and glorious ; and yet man, forsooth, disdains that he is mortal! Oh, mind of ours, inordinate and proud !"

It is true cities and kingdoms die, but the eternal thought lives on. Great thought, incorporate with great action, does not die, but lives a universal life, and its power is felt vibrating through all spirit, and throughout all the ages.

I doubt whether or not we should mourn for any of the dead. I am confident that there should be no mourning for those who render themselves up as sacrifices in any great, just and holy cause. It better becomes us to praise and dignify them.

It was the faith of an ancient people that the souls of heroes did not rest until their great deeds had been hymned by bards, to the sounds of martial music.

Bards, worthy of the ancient time, have hymned the praise of the great citizen, Senator and soldier, who has left us. They have showered on his memory

> " Those leaves, which for the eternal few
>   Who wander o'er the paradise of fame,
> In sacred dedication ever grew."

I would that I were able to add a single leaf to the eternal amaranth.

In long future years, when our night of horror shall have passed, and there shall have come again

> " The welcome morning with its rays of peace,"

young seekers after fame, and young lovers of freedom throughout all this land, yea, and other and distant lands, will recognize, honor, and imitate our late associate as one of the undying dead.

REMARKS OF HON. SCHUYLER COLFAX, IN THE HOUSE OF REPRESENTATIVES.

Mr. Speaker:—The funeral procession of the departed Baker has passed through the crowded streets of our Atlantic cities. The steamer, perhaps, to-day is bearing its precious burden between the portals of the Golden Gate. The thousands who, with enthusiastic acclaim, cheered his departure as a Senator, stand, with bowed frames, and bared heads, and weeping eyes, to. receive with honor, but with sorrow, the lifeless remains that are to be buried in their midst. And there devolves upon us, his former associates, brought by the telegraph almost to the side of his open grave, the duty of rendering also our tribute of affection to his memory.

To say that the deceased Senator was an extraordinary man, is simply to reiterate what the whole country long since conceded. He carved out his own niche in the temple of fame. He built his own pedestal in our American Valhalla. And if the French philosopher, D'Alembert, was correct in saying that there are but three ways of rising in the world—to soar, to crawl and to climb—our friend's history is a striking exemplification of the last and worthiest of these ways. The hand-loom weaver boy of Philadelphia—the friendless lad, with his whole fortune in a meager bundle, turning his face westward—the patient journey, footsore and weary, over mountains and valleys—the deputy in the clerk's office at Carrollton, patiently mastering the principles of the law—his rapid rise in his profession—his election to Congress from the Capital (district) of Illinois—his volunteering in the Mexican war, and raising, equipping, and marching his regiment within fourteen days— his brilliant charge at Cerro Gordo, when, following up the victory which his impetuous and dashing heroism had mainly won, he pursued the enemy for miles with fearful slaughter—his removal, on his return, to another Congressional district, which he carried by his wonderful eloquence against its previous political convictions—his removal to California—his thrilling oration over the murdered Broderick—his triumphant canvass in Oregon—his election to the Senate by a Legis-lature, a large majority of which differed with him in their political associations—his brilliant and impromptu denunciations of traitors, whom, in the Senate Chamber, he prophetically hurled from the Tarpeian rock—his exchanging the robe of the Senator for the sword of the soldier—his daring struggle to wrest victory, against overwhelming odds, from fate itself—and his death at the head of his column, literally with his back to the field and his face to the foe—what an eventful life! to be crowned by such a glorious death.

We know not but that death may have been as welcome to him as life, especially when he fell in such a sacred cause. Some long for death on the battle-field, knowing that it is appointed for all men once to die, and that he who dies for his country is enshrined forever in thousands upon thousands of patriot hearts. Others, who, if we could put a window in their breasts, we would find that they carried a burden of care or sorrow through life, feel that the shaft of death, when sped by its messenger, would have no pain for them. And with others, life is so joyous that the hour of their departure is one of gloom, and thick darkness encompasses the valley their feet must tread. But for our friend, who had won his way to his highest ambition, and who fell, in the very zenith of his fame, in defense of the Constitution and the Union, charging at the head of advancing columns, careless of danger, of odds, or of death, leaving behind him a glory which shall survive long after his tombstone has molded into dust—we should rather weave for him a garland of joy than a chaplet of sorrow.

I know there was sadness in the family, which no earthly sympathy can assuage. I know there was sadness at the White House, where his early friends mourned their irreparable loss. I know there was sadness at the Capitol; sadness on the Atlantic coast; sadness in the valley of the Mississippi; sadness, as one of the first messages flashed along the wire he had so earnestly longed to see stretched from ocean to ocean, bore to the Pacific the tidings of their great loss. There was sadness around the camp-fires of over half a million gallant volunteers, who, like him, had offered their lives to their country in its hour of trial. So, too, if the legends of antiquity intend to commemorate some patriotic sacrifice of life by the story of Curtius leaping into an open gulf to save the Roman republic, was there sorrow doubtless at his fate. And sadness, too, when Leonidas, at the head of his feeble band looked death calmly in the face, and gave up his narrow span o earthly life to live immortalized in history.

But, though there be sadness such as this, let us also rejoice tha our friend has left behind him such a record and such a fame, height ened by his magical eloquence, and hallowed forever by his fervi patriotism. For doubly crowned as statesman and warrior—

"From the top of fame's ladder he stepped to the sky."

www.ingramcontent.com/pod-product-compliance
Lightning Source LLC
Chambersburg PA
CBHW021135020726
47500CB00003B/1095